'Corrie tells me that the two of you crossed swords a few times in your childhood,' Sheila remarked. William roared with laughter.

'I do seem to remember a few occasions,' he said with a sly look at Corrie. 'I had to put her in her place more than once, as I remember.' To her horror he added, 'I've never known such a little tomboy—always tearing her knickers on the brambles trying to keep up with me, weren't you, Corrie?'

'I certainly don't remember *that*,' she said indignantly. Suddenly she felt acutely uncomfortable with this man, this stranger who knew so much about her, as his eyes appraised her with disconcerting frankness from head to foot.

'You used to be such a skinny little kid, but you've filled out quite nicely.' He chuckled at her indignant look. 'Don't be offended, Corrie. We go back a long way, after all, and it was meant as a compliment.'

'Thanks for telling me. I'd never have guessed.'

Sarah Franklin lives in Cambridgeshire with her husband, cat and a 'very bossy but lovable' dog. She has always been interested in anything medical. Both her daughters, before marriage, were working in the field of medicine; one as a nurse, the other as an aesthetician, and Sarah herself has been a keen member of the St John Ambulance Brigade and holds their certificates for nursing and first aid. Writing and researching the medical content of her books takes up most of her time, and her hobbies include gardening, the theatre and music as well as 'dabbling with a paintbrush'.

Previous Titles

GOODBYE TO YESTERDAY
GIVE ME TOMORROW
FAMILY PRACTICE

AFFAIRS OF THE HEART

BY

SARAH FRANKLIN

MILLS & BOON LIMITED
ETON HOUSE   18–24 PARADISE ROAD
RICHMOND   SURREY   TW9 1SR

*First published in Great Britain 1992
by Mills & Boon Limited*

© Sarah Franklin 1992

*Australian copyright 1992
Philippine copyright 1992
This edition 1992*

ISBN 0 263 77524 0

*Set in 10½ on 12 pt Linotron Baskerville
03-9201-52425
Typeset in Great Britain by Centracet, Cambridge
Made and printed in Great Britain*

CHAPTER ONE

As THE night train for Inverness pulled out of Euston Station Corrie leaned out of the window. Watching the lights of London slipping past as the train gathered speed, she was strongly aware that this was a milestone in her life. Not only was she leaving behind the city where she had trained and worked hard for the past six years; she was leaving behind all that she had worked for, her hard-won promotion, her colleagues and patients. But more, much more than that, she was leaving behind for ever the only man she would ever love.

The cool spring air chilled her suddenly and she withdrew into the carriage, pulling up the window. Looking at her watch, she saw that the train had left dead on time. It was two minutes past ten. Soon she would find her sleeper and go to bed. When she woke she would be in Scotland. She tried hard to look forward to the new life that would begin tomorrow, back in Glencarron, the little Highland town where she had grown up. It had been like a stroke of fate, picking up the nursing journal in the sisters' common-room that day and seeing the name 'Glencarron' leaping off the page at her. The mere sight of the name in print instantly evoked memories of the sapphire-blue loch, sparkling in the sunshine, the sharp scents of pine and peat and the crisp tang of crystal-clear mountain air. Reading on, she saw that the advertisement invited applications from a qualified nurse or physiotherapist to care for an elderly lady, newly diagnosed as having multiple sclerosis. It couldn't have come at a more opportune moment for Corrie, and even before she had finished reading she was reaching for a pencil and taking down the box number. The same night she had written off for further details.

Glencarron was her father's birthplace. It was to the Highlands that he himself had retreated when Corrie's mother died. Desolated, he had given up his home and practice in London and taken five-year-old Corrie to Glencarron to set up a practice twenty years ago. He had remained there until his sudden death from a heart attack three years ago.

Walking along the corridor of the swaying train, Corrie found the bar and treated herself to a drink—whisky with plenty of ginger ale, in the hope that it would help her to sleep. A group of businessmen propped up the bar in the narrow compartment, talking and laughing noisily. When she came in they stopped their chatter to eye the slender dark-eyed girl, their expressions ranging from open admiration to insolent speculation. Corrie felt herself flush with annoyance. When *would* a woman be able to go into a bar alone without being made to feel like an insect under a microscope? Avoiding their eyes, she downed her drink and went in search of her sleeper.

Ten minutes later, undressed and lying in the darkness, she found her thoughts turning as usual to Hugh. Not even the motion of the train and the rhythmic rumbling of wheels on track could shut him out, much to her frustrated irritation. When would it stop? When would she be free of him? Every waking moment seemed to be haunted by the memory of what she had fondly imagined they shared—of his subsequent betrayal and insensitivity. Her hands clenched into fists at her sides. '*Damn* you, Hugh,' she whispered into the darkness. 'When will you go away and give me some peace? Surely Glencarron will be far enough away for me to lose you?' But, lying there alone in her narrow berth, she wasn't at all confident that it would.

Closing her eyes, she made herself think about Glencarron and the new job. Her written request for details had brought a response by return of post, and when she opened the letter she had a further surprise. It was signed by Dr Walter Forbes, her father's ex-partner.

My dear Corrie,

I can't tell you how delighted I was to hear from you and to see that you had attained the position of sister since we last met. But, pleasant though it is to hear from you, I'm afraid that the post advertised may not suit a young and ambitious nurse such as yourself. What I really had in mind was an older woman, perhaps a retired nurse or physiotherapist. You will no doubt be surprised to learn that the patient is Mrs Sheila Fraser, who was once your headmistress. She has recently been diagnosed as suffering from MS. As you know, she has always been an extremely active and energetic lady, and at the moment she's inclined to ignore all the advice I've tried to give her. I'm afraid she may not take proper care of herself. She needs someone to help her understand and manage her condition; acquaint her with the daily routine of diet, exercise and rest which at present she finds so tiresome and tends to disregard. Perhaps at the present stage of your career you wouldn't find this kind of work challenging enough. However, if you're still interested I shall be in London next week and will be more than pleased to interview you for the post at my hotel. (Address at the end of this letter.) But even if you're not interested I would still be delighted to see you, so do please get in touch.

Yours, Walter Forbes. (Or do I still qualify for the title 'Uncle Walt'?)

Corrie smiled into the darkness as she remembered her reunion with Uncle Walt. Apart from a thinning of his hair and a thickening of his waistline he was the same as ever, warm and jovial. He welcomed her heartily in the lounge of the quiet Bloomsbury hotel where he always stayed when he was in London. It was three-thirty in the afternoon and the lounge was almost empty. Dr Forbes ordered tea and then reached for Corrie's hands, studying her closely.

'Well now, let me look at you. Mmm—you've grown up,' he pronounced after a moment.

Corrie smiled wryly. 'I'd better have! I'm twenty-five—almost twenty-six.'

He shook his head. 'I can't believe it. It seems just yesterday that your father first brought you to Glencarron, a timid wee girl with a mop of curly hair and great brown eyes too big for your face.' He sighed. 'But then time has a habit of catching us unawares.'

Tea arrived, and as Corrie poured he explained to her about Mrs Fraser.

'When her husband Donald died she gave up teaching and came back to London, which, as you know, was her original home. She took up social work, training as a counsellor. But the pull of the Highlands was stronger than she thought, and she came back to us again a few years later. For the past few years she and I have run a counselling service for the local community.'

'How interesting,' said Corrie. 'Mrs Fraser would make a good counsellor. She was always a very kind, wise person, as I remember. When did she become ill?'

Dr Forbes shook his head. 'Longer ago than she'll admit. I'd noticed more and more how easily she tired. It wasn't like her. Then I spotted other symptoms—a vagueness when she was overtired—again so unlike her; she was always catching colds, then finally she developed a stiffness in one leg. That was when I persuaded her to go into hospital and have some tests. My worst fears were confirmed, I'm afraid. It was MS.'

'Poor Mrs Fraser. What bad luck!'

'She was devastated—just couldn't come to terms with it. To Sheila it was the end of the world. And she absolutely refused to accept that her lifestyle would have to be curtailed. She seemed to think that if she just ignored it, it would simply go away.'

'But surely, with careful management—the right diet and so on—MS sufferers can lead an almost normal life?' queried Corrie.

Dr Forbes smiled. 'Exactly, but I've had a hard

time convincing Sheila of that. Finally she let me talk her into advertising for someone to help her. I can't be watching over her twenty-four hours a day. Besides, I feel she'd take advice better from another woman.' He laughed. 'You know Sheila. On the quiet she thinks most men are tuppence short of a shilling.'

Corrie laughed, remembering the tall, upright woman who had played such as important part in her upbringing and education. Strict and disciplined yet always scrupulously fair, Mrs Fraser had kept her pupils firmly under control, yet she had a lighter side. With affection Corrie recalled the bright blue eyes that could flash with anger or sparkle with charm, and the quirky, biting wit that could take the heat out of the most harrowing situation. 'I imagine she won't be the easiest of patients,' she remarked with a smile.

'That's putting it mildly.' Dr Forbes sipped his tea, regarding her over the rim of the cup. 'Which is why it would be nice to engage someone who knows her— as you do. I'm afraid it could quite well develop into a battle of wills, and it will take a special kind of person not to chicken out, as they say.'

'In spite of what you said, it's sounding more of a challenge by the minute,' Corrie remarked.

Dr Forbes put down his cup and looked at her ruefully. 'Not a job for you, my dear.'

She was dismayed. 'Why do you say that?'

He shook his head. 'You're young. You'll be wanting to further your career, not take time out for what can only be a temporary post. Besides, this is a far cry from theatre work, which is what you've been used to. Then there's Glencarron. Maybe you've forgotten how quiet it is. True, it's livened up a litle since you were there. We even have a Chinese restaurant now, and the Gordon Arms runs a weekly—what do they call it—a disco? But you've been used to all that London has to offer—concerts, museums, theatres. . .'

'All that palls after a while—and I do have a particular reason for wanting a change,' Corrie told him.

He looked up, his perceptive brown eyes searching hers. 'Oh? Nothing wrong, my dear, is there?'

'Oh no,' Corrie said quickly. 'Like Mrs Fraser, I feel the pull of the Highlands too, even though I'm another sassenach. London can be a very tiring place to work.' It wasn't completely true, but she told herself that it would do—for now.

Dr Forbes still looked unsure. 'Well, it goes without saying, Corrie, that I'd rather it were you than anyone I can think of. But I'd have to be convinced that whoever accepted the job would be able to settle for a while. Sheila's well-being is my prime concern, after all.' He smiled at her ruefully. 'Can you just imagine how much she'd enjoy telling me, "I told you so"?'

She promised him she'd take a couple of days to think about it and then drop him a line. But even as she left the hotel that afternoon she already knew that she would accept the job.

She left it two days before she wrote to Dr Forbes. Having thought about it, she decided she must be open and honest with him. After all, he was almost family. In her letter she laid her cards on the table.

Dear Uncle Walt,
    I've thought very carefully about the job, and nothing would please me more than to come to

Glencarron and take care of Mrs Fraser for as long
as she needs me. The fact that the job is temporary
will suit me very well, for reasons which I will try
to explain.

For the past year I have been in love with a
consultant surgeon with whom I work. Unfortu-
nately he's married, so the situation is completely
hopeless and has now come to its inevitable, and
very painful, end. In order to ease the situation and
to get over my unhappiness I must remove myself
as far from him and from my present environment
as I can. However, although it would be lovely to
come 'home' and to be among old friends, I
wouldn't like you to think that the job you offer is
merely an escape route for me. Caring for Mrs
Fraser will be most rewarding. I'm sure we shall
help each other.

Hoping to hear from you soon,

Yours affectionately, Corrie.

As she sealed the envelope she told herself that he
must now make up his own mind. If he thought she
was taking the job for the wrong reasons she was sure
he would say so.

Three days later Corrie arrived back at her flat one
evening after a long shift in the theatre to find the
telephone ringing. Throwing down her bag, she
snatched up the receiver with an exasperated sigh,
hoping it was a wrong number. She wanted nothing
more than a long hot bath, supper and bed.

'Hello, Corinne Ashley?'

'Corrie, my dear! It's Sheila Fraser.'

'Mrs Fraser, what a lovely surprise! How are you?'

'I'm fine—except for this irritating ailment I seem to have picked up. Walter tells me you're coming up to help me work out a routine to lick me back into shape.'

'Well, if that's all right with you,' Corrie agreed.

'My dear, I can't think of anything I'd like better. When Walter first suggested the idea I was horrified. I imagined some sort of *keeper*, a great bossy woman in a starched apron who'd come into my home and order me about. It made me feel so *old*—positively geriatric! But when he told me he'd found you. . .'

Corrie laughed. 'I can't wait to see you again, Mrs Fraser.'

'*Sheila*, please. If you're going to share my home with me we'll have to be on Christian-name terms. I insist. Now listen—this is what I propose. . .' Corrie smiled. It wouldn't be easy, telling Sheila Fraser what to do—or remembering to call her old headmistress by her Christian name. She obviously hadn't changed much, in spite of her illness.

'You're to have two rooms to yourself,' Sheila was saying. 'I won't have you feeling you have to spend all your time tied to me. And to be honest, I might want to be alone myself sometimes. Now, I'm having what used to be Donald's study made into a sitting-room for you. You'll have your own TV, of course, and the use of the car whenever you want it, and of course you'll be free to entertain friends whenever you wish.' She paused. 'I take it you can drive?'

'Oh, yes.'

'That's good. You know what it's like here—if you can't drive you can't go far. So—when can you come?'

'My notice is up next week,' Corrie told her.

'Fine. Then come as soon as you like—and welcome.'

Corrie put down the telephone and stood for a moment looking round the small flat whose empty silence held so many memories. So — it was done. One more week and she would be gone. The segment of her life that had been occupied and dominated by Hugh would be cleanly cut out. Everything they had shared, the traumas and the delights, the tears and the laughter, would be no more than a memory—a sad, aching, bitter-sweet memory.

The train had stopped—perhaps to pick up mail. Corrie woke just as it began to move again. Lights flashed past the window, the rhythm altered, making the train sway and rock. Corrie slipped her legs over the side of the berth and drew on her robe. Out in the corridor she saw that it was just getting light. A cold, pearly sky cast milky shadows over her first glimpse of Scotland. She stood for a moment, watching the craggy landscape slipping past as the train picked up speed again. Opening one of the top windows, she could smell the familiar fragrance of the Highlands on the chill morning air and her heart lifted a little. She was coming home.

Further sleep was out of the question now that she was wide awake, and she lay on top of the berth in her robe, trying to visualise her future. But it seemed that her mind wasn't ready to face it yet. Try as she would, all she could think of was the past—of Hugh and the love that refused to let her go. She'd tried so hard to tell herself how wrong it had been. He was so

much older. He was married. He'd deceived her—
and his wife. He was a liar and a cheat—and an
experienced one at that. She was lucky, *lucky* to have
done with him. But all that was her practical nurse's
mind. Her traitorous woman's heart was another
matter. Swelling painfully until it seemed to fill her
chest and throat, it tortured her with other memories—his voice, deep and slightly husky; the way his
eyes danced when he smiled; the way his hair grew in
the nape of his neck; his kisses and the wonderful,
strong feel of his arms around her. She swallowed
hard at the lump in her throat and brushed angrily at
the single tear that slid down her cheek. Would she
ever be truly free again? Looking at her watch, she saw
that it was almost six o'clock. They would soon be
serving morning tea in the buffet car. She'd get up,
wash and dress. By the time she'd had breakfast they
would be arriving in Inverness.

As the train pulled into the station Corrie was at
the window, scanning the people crowding the plat-
form for the familiar stocky figure. But Dr Walter
didn't seem to be among them. She disembarked, and
as she stood there, surrounded by her luggage, she
looked at her watch. The train was on time. It wasn't
like Uncle Walt to be late. All around her people were
being greeted; gradually they melted away towards
the barrier and the crowd thinned to a mere handful.
She wondered what to do. Glencarron was a long way
off. Would there be a bus? she wondered. She would
summon a porter and ask—get help with her luggage
at least. She turned to pick up the larger of her cases
and, as she bent down, almost collided with a tall
man.

'Oh—I'm sorry.' Her eyes travelled up to look into his face and she caught her breath in surprise.

'Corrie.' He was smiling. 'It is Corrie Ashley, isn't it?'

'Yes, it is.' She stared incredulously. 'But I wasn't expecting to see you.' Dr Walter's son William and she had grown up together in the old far-off days before they both went off to study for their respective careers. But it was years since she had seen him. If he hadn't spoken to her she would never have recognised him. To begin with, he was much taller than she remembered. And he had broadened. The gangling youth with his long arms and bony wrists had grown into a muscular, athletic man, whose shoulders owed nothing to the padding in his tweed jacket. The unruly carrot-red hair had deepened to a rich copper, although she noticed that it still had a tendency to slip forward over his brow. And those freckles. . .they seemed to have joined themselves up into a smooth golden tan. The one thing that hadn't changed was his eyes: grey-green, all-seeing, disconcerting eyes that always seemed able to see right inside her head.

'It's all right, I really am the William you used to know.' Clearly he hadn't lost the knack. She blushed, realising that she had been scrutinising him.

'Of course. I'd have known you anywhere,' she lied, bending and pretending to fuss with her case.

'Well, that's more than I can say for you.' He took the case from her, putting it under his arm and picking up two more. 'I had to wait till almost all the other passengers had gone to be sure—didn't want to be accused of trying to pick up some total stranger. You've changed.'

'Well, it's been a long time.' She followed him, fishing in her handbag for her ticket.

In the car park he hoisted her cases effortlessly into the boot of a bright red BMW Cabriolet, turning to grin at her as he did so.

'Go on—say it,' he said.

'I'm sorry—say what?'

'That it doesn't look like the kind of car for a Highland GP.'

She frowned. 'Is that what you are? I thought you must be home on holiday or something.'

He shook his head. 'Good heavens, didn't Dad tell you? I'm Glencarron's one and only medic. I took over from Dad when he retired.'

Corrie's heart plummeted. The boy who had teased the life out of her all those years ago—later, the first young man to break her tender sixteen-year-old heart. Of all people to find herself working with in her new job. And Uncle Walt must have known it would put her off, which was why he hadn't told her.

As he nosed the car out of the car park William glanced at her, his eyes twinkling. 'Oh dear, I see I've come as a shock.'

She forced herself to smile at him. 'No, of course you haven't. It is a surprise, though. And it's odd that Uncle Walt didn't think it important enough to mention.'

He laughed. 'That's because he hasn't quite let go yet. As a matter of fact, he's taking surgery for me this morning, to give me this chance to meet you and have a chat. And of course he was Sheila Fraser's good friend and doctor long before I was, which was why he took on the task of finding a nurse for her.'

'Yes—I see.'

They drove in silence as William skilfully negotiated the heavy morning traffic in the town centre. Corrie glanced at his strong profile and memories came flooding back. William had made her life a perfect misery when they were children. Four years older and highly innovative at practical joking, he never missed a trick. She shuddered, remembering the slugs in her lunch box; the habit he had of concealing himself in trees, waiting for her to pass beneath so that he could drop sticky burrs in her thick curly hair. She recalled the anguish she had felt when he had hidden her brand new bicycle and made her late for school, and many other uncomfortable and humiliating occasions. But none of them had stopped her secretly hero-worshipping him. Even now she blushed to think of the shameless way she had pursued him—until at last he had wounded her too deeply for redemption; broken her heart by taking her best friend Christie Mackenzie to the Christmas dance when she had expected him to take her. That first intolerable pain of rejection was something she would never forget. She had sworn then and there to hate William Forbes for the rest of her days.

'Are you all right? You're looking rather pensive,' William remarked as they reached the outskirts of the town.

She swallowed the memories and adjusted her expression carefully. 'Yes, thank you, I'm fine.' But in her heart she was far from fine. Coming here to get over Hugh's heartless treatment, only to be confronted by a chunk of her past she would rather forget, was far from ideal. She supposed she'd just have to make the best of it.

The journey from Inverness to Glencarron took two and a half hours. Even William's powerful BMW could not make it in a shorter time. The mountain roads were narrow and at times it was necessary to back into one of the passing places to let another vehicle pass, but Corrie found herself enjoying it. The spring morning was bright and fresh, the higher slopes were still dappled with snow that glittered in the sunshine, and she drank in the scenery and the clear air hungrily. It tasted and smelt so good after London. As they drove she began to relax, and when William started to talk about Sheila Fraser's medical condition she welcomed the chance to learn all she could.

'I've been reading up on MS,' she told him. 'I haven't come across that many cases during my nursing, but I found quite a few books on it in the hospital library. Is Mrs Fraser much affected?'

'There's the characteristic fatigue, which was the first telltale symptom. And the fact that she seems to pick up every little germ that's going, besides the other things Dad will have told you about. But I think what really frightens her is the loss of memory she experiences sometimes. I can't convince her that it wouldn't happen if she didn't allow herself to become overtired. As you know, it's a progressive disease, which is why I'm anxious to get her on to a suitable regimen as soon as possible. She's one of those unfortunate people who reacts badly to steroid treatment.'

'Has she tried a gluten-free diet?'

William shook his head. 'I sidetracked that by having some allergy tests done while she was at the hospital. As you know, that diet is based on allergies. But she doesn't seem to be allergic to anything, which is just as well. It might have proved difficult up here, getting supplies of gluten-free flour and so on.'

'There are several others. I've brought some books with me,' Corrie told him. 'It might be as well to begin by concentrating on foods rich in essential fatty acids.'

William turned to smile at her. 'Mmm, you have done your homework well, haven't you? All you have to do now is convince Sheila.'

It was almost eleven o'clock when Corrie saw the mountain road beginning to drop away before them and caught her first glimpse of sparkling blue water in the distance. She felt her heart quicken.

'Lochbawn—how beautiful it looks in the sunshine.'

'Yes, we'll be home soon.' William lifted one hand from the wheel and laid it briefly on her arm. 'I hope you'll find happiness again here with us, Corrie.'

She turned to look at him, her eyes startled. What did he mean by that? Surely Uncle Walt couldn't have told him what was in her letter? 'I'm sure I will,' she said.

Although ahead of them on the winding road she could see the cluster of little whitewashed houses that made up the small fishing port of Glencarron, William turned off the road before they reached it to follow a narrow track that ran beside the loch. She turned to him in surprise.

'Mrs Fraser still lives at Glencoe House, then?'

'Oh, yes. I can't imagine her living anywhere else, can you?'

'But when she went back to London. . .?'

'Ah, I see what you mean. No, she didn't sell up, just let the place out during the time she was away, which was just as well.' He smiled. 'It was here waiting for her like an old friend when she came back.'

By now Corrie could see the house. Long, low and whitewashed like the other houses, it sat on a little knoll in the shadow of the mountain overlooking the loch. A little burn bubbled and sang over smooth boulders as it passed the house on its way to the loch. Sheila had once explained that the knoll on which the house stood had been formed by peat, brought across the Irish Sea many years ago by fishermen who used it as ballast for the empty boats they would fill with herring. On this rich soil Sheila had created her beloved garden. Blazing with every spring flower imaginable, it made a splash of bright colour against the sombre pine-clad backcloth of the mountain landscape.

The house was reached by a flight of shallow stone steps, and as they drew closer Corrie saw a tall slim figure come out through the open front door to stand at the top of the steps, shading her eyes from the powerful sunlight as she watched their approach.

'There—look!' she said excitedly. 'It's Mrs Fraser. She must have seen us coming.'

As the car drew to a halt and Corrie got out Sheila came down the steps to meet them. She looked a little older, and Corrie immediately noticed the slight stoop of her shoulders and the stiffness in her legs, but the blue eyes sparkled with pleasure as she held out both hands.

'Corinne Ashley, my favourite head girl! Welcome to Glencoe House,' she said in the soft Scottish accent she had acquired.

Corrie laughed and shook her head as she took the slim, strong hands in hers. 'If you're to be Sheila I'll be Corrie, if you don't mind. And we can forget the head girl bit too?'

Sheila laughed with her. 'Of course—you're right. From now on we're friends—equals.'

William joined them. 'Except when you're doing as she tells you, Sheila,' he said. 'Which I sincerely hope will be all the time.'

The two women looked at each other gravely, quietly assessing one another.

'I promise you there isn't one starched apron in my luggage,' Corrie said gravely. 'And if I develop a bossy manner you can sack me on the spot.'

'Just you dare,' warned William, wagging his finger at Sheila. 'After all the trouble I've gone to you two had just better hit it off!'

In the long, low-ceilinged sitting-room of Glencoe House, with its wonderful view over the loch, Sheila had coffee and freshly baked scones waiting.

'You'll stay and take some with us, William?' she asked, but he shook his head.

'I've an appointment at half-eleven.' He looked at his watch. 'I'll be hard pushed to make it as it is. Anyway, I'm sure you two have plenty of talking to do.' He grinned at Sheila, his eyes twinkling in the wicked way that Corrie remembered so well. 'Tell you what, though, I might come to lunch, if you were to ask me nicely.'

'Nothing like inviting yourself, is there?' laughed Sheila. 'All right, then—one o'clock sharp. And don't keep us waiting.'

Corrie walked back to the car with him. 'If you just leave the last of my cases here I'll bring it up later. And thanks for meeting me.'

'Not at all. The least I could do.' He started the engine and turned to smile at her. 'See you later, then.'

Corrie watched as the BMW bumped over the rough track, winding its way back to the road, her mind working overtime. William Forbes was the last person she had expected to be working with. Although she had to admit that on the face of it he had grown up and was now a responsible, mature man and a doctor, in her mind she would always see him as that maddening red-haired youth who had blighted her formative years. With a sigh she picked up the last of her cases and headed back towards the house. There was nothing for it but to make the best of a bad job and to behave like a dignified adult woman, she told herself.

In the sitting-room Sheila was pouring fragrant coffee into wafer-thin china cups as Corrie returned. 'I can't tell you how pleased I am to have you here, dear,' she said, passing her a cup. 'We shall be able to chat about old times. And I want to hear all you've been doing in London.'

Corrie sipped her coffee thoughtfully. 'It was quite a shock, discovering that William is your doctor,' she said.

'But didn't Walter tell you?' asked Sheila.

'No, as a matter of fact he didn't.'

'Well, it isn't surprising. You know, I don't think he's quite come to terms with his retirement yet, though of course he was so proud to have William take over from him.' Sheila regarded Corrie thoughtfully. 'Why was it such a shock, though?'

'William and I used to quarrel dreadfully as children,' Corrie explained.

Sheila laughed. 'He *was* a mischievous boy, wasn't he? And then later, as a medical student—changing his girlfriends as often as his socks.' She shook her head. 'Too fond of good time, I told myself. I couldn't really see him settling down in a place like Glencarron. I confess I wondered what kind of doctor he would make. But I've no complaints. He's so dedicated. He's the perfect successor to his father. I couldn't want a better doctor.'

When they had finished their coffee Sheila showed Corrie her new accommodation. As Glencoe House had once been two cottages it boasted two staircases. The one at the far end of the house had belonged to the smaller of the two cottages, and the rooms above now formed a small suite of rooms, one of which Donald Fraser, headmaster of the local primary school, had used as a study. Now it was furnished charmingly with two chintz-covered armchairs, a table, TV and a desk. Off this was a long, low-ceilinged bedroom whose window overlooked the mountains and loch.

'There's a little bathroom just along the passage,' Sheila told her. 'And you have your own entrance—

as long as you don't mind coming in through the back.'

Corrie exclaimed with delight. 'Is all this for me? There's no need, really.'

'Of course there is, my dear. I want you to be happy here and to feel you have a measure of independence.' They were looking out of the landing window as she spoke, facing the track that led down from the road, when suddenly a car came into view. Sheila drew in her breath sharply.

'Oh, would you believe it? Here's William back already. Come along, my dear. We'd better go down.'

Over a pre-lunch sherry Sheila glanced at the two young people opposite her and thought what a handsome couple they made. 'Corrie tells me the two of you crossed swords a few times in your childhood,' she remarked, much to Corrie's embarrassment.

William roared with laughter. 'I do seem to remember a few occasions,' he said with a sly grin at Corrie. 'I had to put her in her place more than once, as I remember.' To her horror he added, 'I've never known such a little tomboy—always tearing her knickers on the brambles trying to keep up with me, weren't you, Corrie?'

'I certainly don't remember *that*,' she said indignantly.

He chuckled. 'Ah well, we deliberately forget the things that are too undignified to remember, don't we?' He turned to Sheila. 'Well now, how are you? Maybe we'd better all three of us have a good chinwag and work out some sort of routine for you now that Corrie is here.' He looked at his watch. 'Will lunch be long?'

Sheila laughed. 'Nothing like laying down the law, is there? A good thing I know you so well, William Forbes.' She got to her feet. 'You two go through to the dining-room while I tell Kathy we're ready to eat.'

Corrie walked ahead of him into the dining-room and perched on the arm of a chair near the window. Suddenly she felt acutely uncomfortable with this man, this stranger who knew so much about her. 'It's a wonderful view from this window,' she said. Turning, she caught him looking at her with an odd little half-smile.

'It's not so bad from here either.' His eyes appraised her with disconcerting frankness from head to foot. 'You used to be such a skinny little kid, but you've filled out quite nicely—in all the right places too.' He chuckled at her indignant look. 'Don't look so offended, Corrie. We go back an awful long way, after all. And it was meant as a compliment.'

'Thanks for telling me. I'd never have guessed.'

He winced. 'Ouch! You're still cross with me for saying you tore your knickers, aren't you?'

'I usually disregard any such juvenile remarks. Anyway, I'm sure it isn't true.' She turned her hot face away from him to look out of the window again. It really was too bad. He hadn't really changed at all. She'd come here to forget about one insensitive man, only to be confronted with awful, irritating William Forbes. And to think she'd be obliged to work with him too! Suddenly her throat tightened and tears stung her eyes. It wasn't fair. It just wasn't fair!

'By the way, the letter you wrote to Dad—I passed

it on.' The casual remark dropped into the silence like a stone into a pool.

Her head spun round and her cheeks grew even hotter. She had addressed Uncle Walt's letter to the surgery—not realising that he had retired—to Dr W. Forbes, care of the surgery. As William was the only Dr W. Forbes there now *he* must have opened and read it. That would explain his remark in the car earlier—about hoping she'd find happiness here. She felt her face grow hot, remembering her outpourings about her unhappy love affair with Hugh. What a field day William could have with that juicy little piece of information if he chose! Her startled eyes searched his for some sign of triumph.

'My letter? You—you passed it on?'

'Yes, as I said. . .' His eyes held hers, revealing nothing. But she thought she detected a glint of the old mischief in them. 'Yes,' he repeated, 'I passed it on to Dad as soon as I realised the mistake, naturally.'

CHAPTER TWO

KATHY MACDONALD came in to do the housework at Glencoe House each morning and to prepare lunch. She had already laid lunch for two in the dining-room, but she happily laid another place when she knew it was for Dr William. As he had delivered her first grandchild just four years ago he could do no wrong as far as she was concerned.

In the dining-room the sound of the burn reached them through the open window as they sat eating their lunch. William paid full justice to Kathy's delicious home-cured ham accompanied by tiny new potatoes and a mixed salad. When she came in afterwards with a piping hot apple pie and a jug of cream his eyes lit up.

'Kathy MacDonald, you're a queen among women,' he told her, grinning at her delighted blush. 'There's no one in the whole of Scotland can make an apple pie like yours.'

Corrie winced. Did he really have to pile it on like that? And did Kathy MacDonald really have to behave as though she were falling for his blatant flattery? She was quite relieved when they reached the coffee stage and he raised the subject of Sheila's routine at last.

'Right, now, down to business. First—exercise. I've arranged for a physiotherapist to come in and devise and show you a series of exercises to follow each day.'

Sheila winced. 'Physical jerks? Not my scene. Besides, I'll never remember how to do them.'

'Corrie will see to that,' William told her firmly. 'And physical jerks, as you call them, will have to be part of your daily routine from now on if you want to carry on a normal life. What's wrong, anyway? You want to keep your fine figure, don't you? Want to stay young and beautiful? This way you'll be helping your MS too—keeping your muscles in order.' He glanced at Corrie as though for support. She took the cue.

'That's right. You see, your muscles aren't getting the messages your brain is sending them as efficiently as before,' she said. 'Think of MS as a telephone exchange that's working on half-power. You sometimes need to write a letter to make sure the message gets through. You have to exercise your muscles to remind them of what they should be doing.'

Sheila pulled a face. 'It sounds depressingly like cracking up to me.'

'Not at all,' said William. 'Sheila Fraser, cracking up? That'll be the day! But you'll need to help yourself a bit too. Corrie has some diet ideas.'

Sheila winced again. 'Now *there* I draw the line. I never could stay on a diet. Anyway, I don't think I need to lose weight.'

'The one I have in mind to try first is designed to help build muscle and healthy tissue, not lose weight,' Corrie explained. 'It concentrates on foods rich in essential fatty acids.'

'Urgh! What are they? They sound perfectly revolting.'

'Not nearly as bad as you think,' Corrie assured

her. 'To begin with, oil of evening primrose forms part of it—taken in capsule form. I've brought a supply with me. Then it's a matter of using polyunsaturated oils for cooking and taking plenty of fresh fruit and vegetables. That isn't so bad, is it?'

Sheila looked suspicious. 'And what's the snag? What do I have to go without?'

'Well—cakes and biscuits, cream and butter—most animal fats generally. The apple pie we've just eaten would be out, I'm afraid. But a nice fresh fruit salad would taste just as good, wouldn't it?'

Sheila sighed. 'Mmm. Maybe.'

'But the plus is in the way it helps,' Corrie told her. 'Not so many colds and sniffles, less stiffness and better mobility, improved eyesight, skin and hair. Quicker healing. . .'

'All right, all right, you win,' Sheila laughed good-naturedly. 'We'll give it a whirl, as they say. At this rate the two of you'll have me entering for Miss World before the year is out!'

'And rest,' William put in. 'Now that is *most* important. At least an hour after lunch each day—properly, mind. On the bed with your feet up. Will you promise me that?'

'She will,' Corrie said firmly. 'I shall see to it personally.'

'What about my work—my counselling?' Sheila protested.

'Rearrange your schedule to fit in,' William told her. 'You could even knock five minutes off each appointment so that you get in the same number of people. It's all a matter of organisation.'

'My work isn't quite like that, William,' Sheila

admonished. 'You can't rush people in and out. Sometimes you have to give them twice the time you've allocated to get them to open up.'

'I know, I know.' William looked at Corrie. 'Maybe Corrie here could help with some of the counselling.'

'Now that *is* a good idea.' Sheila looked at her. 'Would you like that?'

Corrie was taken aback. 'Well, I don't know if I could. . .'

'It's largely a matter of just listening,' Sheila told her. 'And in some cases you'd probably be better at inviting confidences than Walter or me. With some of the younger people, for instance—they'd be more likely to open up with someone of their own age group.'

'And Corrie's a woman of the world now,' William put in. 'She's lived in London, tasted life in the fast lane. That experience must be worth something.'

Corrie glanced up at him sharply. What was he getting at? Was he laughing at her? Was it a snide reference to the contents of the letter she had written his father? She felt her cheeks burning again and dropped her gaze as his eyes met hers across the table.

'Isn't that so, Corrie?' he pressed. 'I'm sure your years of training and working in a famous London hospital will have shown you more of life than the average young woman in Glencarron would experience in a lifetime.'

'I'm not at all sure that's true,' she said crisply. 'Anyway, aren't we getting away from what we were discussing?'

William glanced at his watch and exclaimed, 'Ye gods, look at the time! I'll have to be on my way. I should have been at the ante-natal clinic five minutes ago. Start the diet, Corrie. I think it's an excellent idea. And don't forget to rest, Sheila.' He rose from the table. 'And I'll be sending the physio along tomorrow morning. I think you know her, by the way, Corrie. Her name is Christie Mackenzie.'

Corrie's head snapped up. '*Christie*? We were best friends at school. It'll be lovely to see her again. We used to share everything.'

William laughed. 'So I remember,' he chuckled. '*So I remember*.'

Corrie was still glaring at him when Sheila said, 'Well, we mustn't keep you, William. Perhaps when Corrie has settled in you'll take her out and show her around?'

'Oh, no, I. . .' Corrie began, but William forestalled her.

'I intend to.' The clear green stare was insolently teasing. 'Just as soon as she's had time to adjust we'll paint Glencarron red—or at least a subtle shade of puce. Mustn't shock the natives too much with your wicked London ways, must we, Corrie?'

As they stood at the top of the steps, watching the car make the upward climb to the road, Sheila said, 'You mustn't mind William's teasing, dear. It's just his way.'

Corrie smiled wryly. 'I grew up with him, remember? When I was a child he was the bane of my existence. He doesn't seem to have changed much.'

Sheila's eyes clouded as she turned to look at Corrie. 'Oh, dear! I did so hope you two would get along. He had a bad time, you know, as a boy; losing his mother when he was just nine.'

'I lost my mother too,' Corrie reminded her. 'And I came here to a strange place where everything and everyone was new and unfamiliar.'

'And now you've come back, so it can't have been as bad as all that, can it?' Sheila smiled and squeezed her arm. 'Welcome home, dear. I meant to say it when you arrived.'

Corrie smiled, feeling ashamed of grumbling about William after the welcome she'd had. 'Thank you. Take no notice of me. William and I will shake down, I dare say. And now it's time for your rest. Off you go. I'll call you in exactly one hour. In the meantime I'll help Kathy with the washing-up and then I'll unpack.'

Kathy was quite scandalised at the idea of Corrie helping her. 'Away with you, Miss Ashley. I'm paid to do it,' she said. 'I'm sure you have all your unpacking to see to.'

But Corrie was already drying the pile of dishes on the draining board. 'Nonsense! I might need *your* help while I'm here. Tell me about Glencarron and your family.' She needed to have Kathy as an ally and meant to introduce the subject of Sheila's new diet into the conversation tactfully. Some cooks didn't take kindly to being told what to make, and she needed to know just how sensitive Kathy might be on the subject.

'If it wasn't for Mrs Fraser I'd have had to move from here when my Angus was killed at the fishing four years ago,' Kathy said in her soft Highland accent. 'There aren't many jobs for an untrained middle-aged woman in Glencarron. And I did want to stay close to Moira, especially with the baby coming.'

'Moira—that's your daughter?' queried Corrie.

'Aye,' Kathy smiled. 'Such a happy wee family, she and her husband Ian, and wee Angus—named for his grandad.' She emptied the washing-up bowl and wiped it thoughtfully. 'Will Mrs Fraser have to go away for treatment?'

'No,' Corrie told her. 'I'm afraid there's no actual cure for MS. But there are ways of managing it so that she can lead a full and active life free from distressing symptoms—just as long as we can get her to do as she's told.'

Kathy laughed. 'That'll no' be easy! But if I can help, I'll back you and the doctor up all I can.' She sighed. 'A bonny man, Dr William. His father all over again. He was just wonderful when wee Angus was born. He was the first baby Dr William delivered when he came home to take over from his father, you know.' She shook her head. 'And such a difficult birth. My poor wee girl was almost three days in labour. If it hadn't been for Dr William. . .' She eyed Corrie thoughtfully. 'Mrs Fraser says you and he grew up together. Is that a fact?'

'It is. My father was a doctor too—Dr Walter's partner in those days.'

'Aye, I remember Dr Ashley well. He was a fine man too.'

'But Dr William and I have hardly set eyes on each other since we both went away to study,' Corrie told her. 'He never seemed to be at home at the same time as me. Kathy. . .' Corrie decided she must take the plunge and broach the subject she had come to talk about. 'Kathy, Mrs Fraser will be on a special diet from tomorrow onwards. I'd like to explain it to you. It's really very simple and healthy—so much so that I might as well eat what she does. That'll make things easier for you.'

To Corrie's relief Kathy was eager to help and not at all inflexible in her ideas about cooking. It was arranged that she should make the main meal for them at lunchtime and Corrie would manage something simple for their supper.

'No more of the scones she loves so much?' Kathy said regretfully.

'I'm afraid not. But if it's for her good it's best, isn't it? And I'm sure you'll devise some dishes she'll enjoy just as much.'

When the washing-up was finished they sat down together at the kitchen table and Kathy wrote down a list of the foods Sheila was allowed and those that she wasn't. When she had finished she put the list into her handbag.

'I'll sit down with that this evening and work out some nice meals,' she said. 'It'll be quite a challenge.'

'So you don't mind?' said Corrie with some relief. 'I was afraid you might find it tiresome.'

Kathy was taking down her coat from the hook behind the back door. 'There's nothing I wouldn't do to help Mrs Fraser,' she said. 'When Angus was killed I almost gave up. He was my whole life, you see— especially after Moira got married. I couldn't seem to take an interest in anything. It felt like the end of the world. I made myself quite ill—couldn't eat or sleep, couldn't settle to anything. Someone suggested that Dr William might give me some tablets, but he sent me to see Mrs Fraser instead. She made me see that I must pick up the pieces, go on and make a new life for myself—that I still had a lot to offer.' She smiled. 'I'll never forget her kindness to me.'

When Kathy had gone Corrie stood for a long time at the kitchen window. The mountain Craecuillin rose at the back of the house, standing like a benign giant in the sunlight to stand sentinel over the little house. But standing there, Corrie shivered suddenly, imagining how bleak and forbidding it might look on colder, greyer days. She turned abruptly and glanced at the kitchen clock. Kathy and she had talked longer than she'd thought. Sheila had been resting for more than an hour now. She filled the kettle and plugged it in. She would wake her with a cup of tea.

Lying in bed that night, with a melon-coloured full moon shining in at her window and the burn splashing and chuckling, Corrie thought about Kathy's words. Losing someone you loved was hard—she knew that. Hugh hadn't died, but the hurt was no less. In some ways it was worse. It hurt so unbearably, thinking of him going happily about his life without her; enjoying the things he shared with Lucille, his wife; unconcerned by her absence, not even knowing or caring that she still missed him and hurt so badly—in spite of what he'd done.

Closing her eyes, she remembered the day they had first met. It had been her first day as theatre sister. A heart bypass operation. Martin Jessop, the anaesthetist, had introduced them briefly, but all she could see of him as he stood across the operating table from her was his eyes over the green mask. Unusual eyes of sharp, compelling ice blue, concentrating so deeply on his work that he appeared to see nothing else. She watched fascinated as his skilful hands completed the work that would give the patient new life, admiring his brilliance and single-mindedness. Later he came to find her. She remembered his words exactly.

'Sister Ashley, isn't it? I believe this was your first day as a theatre sister. Congratulations. I'm lucky to get such an efficient TS. I'm sure we shall work well together.'

She had been taken aback that he, one of the hospital's most eminent cardiac consultants, should bother to seek her out, even more taken aback by the vibrant attraction he seemed to emanate from every pore. Tall and broad, his muscular arms bare in the greens he still wore, there was a powerful presence— an air of authority. Without the mask, she saw that he was perhaps forty-five or -six. His hair was dark brown, frosted with silver where it swept smoothly back over his ears. But the ice-blue eyes were his most striking feature. They had an almost hypnotic gaze that held her helplessly captive.

When he had first asked her out to dinner two weeks later she had accepted eagerly. His goodnight kiss had completely devastated her. No one had ever kissed her like that before. Within weeks they were dating regularly, and Hugh had become her lover within a month. The first blow came when she had learned that he was married. A staff nurse from Men's Surgical had told her, not without some relish, that she had seen him *with his wife* at the hospital garden party a few weeks previously.

For three weeks Corrie had refused to speak to him.

Her flatmate had advised her to apply for another job, but she had refused, telling herself she would get over it—that she would not allow a man like Hugh to force her out of the job she had worked so hard for. What she knew deep in her heart, but refused to admit, was that life without a daily sighting of him was totally unthinkable, whatever he had done.

At last he cornered her in the corridor one day. She turned a corner and there he was, blocking her path. She was obliged to speak to him.

'I—I'm in a hurry. May I please pass?'

He caught her shoulders. 'Corrie, look at me.'

'Please—I don't want to,' she protested.

'Yes, you do. We have to talk. Meet me for dinner this evening?'

'No.'

Without a word he opened the door and pushed her inside an office. 'Right, now you're going to listen, whether you want to or not.'

'Please, Hugh, let me go. There's nothing to say. Besides, someone might come in.'

He turned the key in the lock. 'Now they won't. Anyway, this happens to be *my* office, so what the hell?' Again he grasped her shoulders. 'Someone has told you about Lucille—right?'

'Your wife—yes.'

An expression of pain filled his eyes. 'Oh, God, I'd rather anything than this, Corrie. I'd have told you myself, but I knew you wouldn't understand. Look our marriage is over. It's been over for years. We've stayed together for the sake of appearances, that's all.' He watched the tears well up in her eyes and pulled her close. 'You know what? I'm *glad* you know. I don't have to pretend any more. Don't refuse to see me, Corrie, I love you—you're all I ever wanted in a woman. I can't lose you now. We met at the wrong time, that's all. Look, I'll tell Lucille I want a divorce.' He held her away from him to look down into her eyes. 'Will you marry me, darling?'

Her throat was too tight for words. All she could whisper as she melted against him was, 'Oh—*Hugh*!' And when his lips found hers all the anguish and resentment she had suffered seemed to dissolve into thin air.

Soon after that she had moved out of the flat and into a larger one that Hugh had found. He joined her there whenever he could. Life was spent in a constant state of uncertainty, soaring highs and desolate lows. She lost most of her friends because she would never arrange to see any of them in case Hugh might be free. Holidays and days off were spent alone, sitting hopefully by the telephone. Disappointments were shattering and many. To those who knew her, she was either in the depths of gloom or on cloud nine. But for Corrie the time they spent together made up for everything. When she was with Hugh nothing else seemed to matter. She was happy, so blissfully happy. Until. . .

When Corrie wakened, she couldn't remember, just at first, where she was. Then she heard the sound of water and all at once she knew. *Glencarron*. Outside her window the water of the loch was painted with silver as the first rays of the sun touched it. The sky was a pale, milky blue and all around were the sounds of early morning. She heard the nasal grunt of a distan stag, hunting for breakfast on the sparse slopes of the mountain, and the high, thin notes of a lark as it soared above, a tiny speck in the high blue haze. She showered and dressed quickly, then went downstairs to find Kathy already in the kitchen.

'I've taken Mrs Fraser her morning tea,' she said. 'I want to make an early start today. I'll have to take the bus into town and buy in the new foods Mrs Fraser needs for the diet. We're to have another visitor, I hear.'

'Miss Mackenzie, the physiotherapist. She's going to devise an exercise programme for Mrs Fraser.'

Kathy turned to give her a wry smile. 'The best of luck to the both of you,' she said. 'I'll do the sitting-room first, then you can take her in there.'

When Sheila came down she was wearing a cotton tracksuit. 'I thought this would be the best wear for this exercise programme,' she said with a smile. 'To tell you the truth, I'm glad to be getting some use from it again. I used to wear it for the garden or my early morning walk, but since I've been stricken with this wretched ailment I haven't felt like doing much of either.'

'Well, maybe you soon will again,' Corrie told her. 'We'll just take one day at a time and see how we go. Don't expect too much all at once.'

Christie arrived at ten-thirty, driving her little blue Mini carefully along the track and drawing up at the bottom of the steps. Corrie had been watching for her and now she went down to meet her. Christie looked much the same. Tall and willowy, her long blonde hair worn in a neat chignon, she looked lean, athletic and businesslike. She took one look at the girl coming to meet her and held out her arms.

'*Corrie*! How marvellous to see you! I've heard all about you from William.'

The girls exchanged hugs and Corrie asked suspiciously, 'What did he say about me?'

Christie laughed. 'Oh, that you were beautiful and haughty, but that he suspected you were as maddening as ever.'

'His cheek! Did he tell you he barged in yesterday before I'd time to unpack and invited himself to lunch?'

Christie leaned into the back of the car for her bag. 'We'll have to have a get-together so that you can fill me in with all your news,' she said. 'I'm dying to hear all about London. Though I must say it's as though you've never been away.'

In the sitting-room Christie put Sheila through a series of gentle exercises, testing and examining the strength of her muscles before she decided on which would be the most beneficial. Later, over coffee, she made out a simple list, leaving Corrie a book with diagrams in which she had marked the relevant ones.

'We'll begin gently with these,' she said. 'Let me know if you want any help or advice. I'll be back in a couple of weeks to see how you're getting on.' She looked at Sheila. 'How's the counselling going? Are you still working?'

'Walter made me take this week off,' Sheila told her. 'I think he thought that beginning my new regimen would be quite enough for me to cope with.' She sighed. 'Anyone would think I had one foot in the grave! I can't tell you how annoying it is. I can't believe that my legs won't be as they've always been—then the moment I try to do things. . .'

'I know.' Christie patted her sholder. 'But trust us, Sheila. The three of us will get you going. Take it easy, be patient and you'll see.'

As Corrie walked back to the car with her Christie said, 'I wonder if this is going to work. Sheila's an impatient, irascible lady. She likes to see immediate results.'

'That's one of the reasons I'm here,' Corrie told her. 'I shall just have to try to divert her. It's a good thing she has her counselling to keep her occupied.'

'She doesn't want to do too much of that either,' Christie warned. 'It can be mentally exhausting.' As she got into the car she asked, 'What about meeting me for a drink at the Gordon Arms this evening? They're having some Highland songs from the local choir.'

'I'd like that,' said Corrie. 'I'll see how Sheila is and let you know.'

When she went back to the house she found Sheila slumped in a chair, looking depressed. 'Are you all right? Were the exercises too much for you?' she asked anxiously.

Sheila shook her head. 'I can't see me ever being the same again,' she said huskily. 'I've tried so hard to tell myself that I'm no different, but I can't go on kidding myself any longer.' She sighed. 'Look at me! I'm a wreck!'

Corrie went to sit on the arm of the chair. She took Sheila's hand and held it tightly. 'Life changes all the time, Sheila. Things happen to us—bad things some-times, things that we can see no good in, however hard we try. But I believe there *is* some good in everything that happens, even though we can't always see it.'

'I wish I could think of just one good thing,' Sheila said despondently.

'Well, to begin with, this experience will help you to understand other people so much better. Once you've come to terms with it, it will make you better at your job.'

'But I *hate* it so. I hate the way I am now. I can feel my limbs letting me down—hear myself getting crotchety and awkward with others—snapping. How can I help people when I'm like that? I'm always telling other people not to be negative, yet just look at *me* when it comes to the crunch!'

Corrie smiled. 'Just do as Christie says and take it easy. You're only feeling negative because you're angry with yourself; angry with your body because it's let you down. What you have to do is learn to like yourself again. Just for the time being, forget others and concentrate on getting to know and like *you* again.'

Sheila looked up at her with a faintly surprised expression. 'You really have grown up, haven't you, Corinne Ashley? You know what it is to be unhappy too, don't you? You've known sadness—I can see it in your eyes. Maybe you'll tell me all about it in your own good time?'

Corrie nodded. 'That's the Sheila Fraser I used to know,' she said. 'Interested in other people's problems—wanting to help. And maybe I will tell you all about myself one day soon. In the meantime I think

Kathy has lunch ready, and I don't know about you, but I'm starving!'

When Sheila had had her rest she was herself again. And when she heard that Christie had invited Corrie to join her at the Gordon Arms that evening she insisted she must go.

'Take the car,' she said. 'It's a tidy walk into town, and coming home along that track in the dark can be hazardous.'

Sheila's car was an ancient Rover, ponderous and heavy, but at least the springs were good and it held the rough track without bumping too much.

Corrie made sure that Sheila was comfortable, her feet up in front of the TV, before she went to change. She put on her favourite dress of soft wool in a shade of poppy red that suited her dark colouring, pulled on a black jacket and went out to the car.

The Gordon Arms was already full when she arrived. The Highland girls' choir had assembled. Wearing their long plaid skirts and tartan sashes over white blouses, they stood round the piano and sang the old songs that Corrie had grown up with. As they were singing when she arrived she stood by the door until they had finished. She spotted Christie almost at once sitting across the room, and after a moment the other girl saw her and waved. The moment the song was finished she beckoned to her. But before Corrie could begin to cross the room a voice behind her said, 'So you've found your way to the pub? That didn't take long, did it? I said you'd developed wicked London habits.'

William stood behind her, leaning on the bar, a

mug of beer in his hand. He grinned. 'Don't look so dismayed! Surely you haven't forgotten my teasing?'

'No, I hadn't. I just hoped you'd have grown out of it by now.'

He took her arm and drew her towards him. 'Well, I'll tell you what. Buy me a drink and your dark secrets are safe.'

'What are you talking about?' She blushed scarlet.

He threw back his head and laughed. 'Ah, hit the nail on the head, have I?'

'I'm sorry, William, but I'm meeting someone,' she said stiffly. Turning, she threaded her way across the room to where Christie sat with a fair-haired young man in jeans and a sweater.

'Hi there, Corrie. Glad you could make it. This is Peter Sinclair—he's a fellow physio. We trained together.'

Corrie shook hands. 'Hello, it's nice to meet you.' But she'd scarcely had time to sit down when William joined them, lowering his tall frame into the seat next to hers. He put a glass of lager on the table in front of Corrie.

'Here, I hope this is to your taste.' He smiled around at them all. 'Well now, isn't this nice?'

Corrie glared at him.

'Thank you, William?' he prompted.

She blushed. 'Ah—oh, yes, thanks—for the drink.'

'I asked William to wait for you over by the bar,' Christie explained, 'and tell you we'd saved some seats.'

'Then why didn't you?' Corrie asked him accusingly.

He took a leisurely drink of his beer, then looked at

her, one eyebrow raised. 'You didn't give me much of a chance,' he said. 'You were too anxious to get away.'

'*You* were too busy making. . .' Corrie broke off. It would be rude and embarrassing to start arguing with William in front of the others. She took a quick sip of her lager. 'I—er—think we have Sheila's routine sorted out,' she said brightly. 'Kathy has a diet in hand and I'm sure she won't find the exercises too difficult.'

She turned to Christie and soon the girls were chatting about old times. Once she had relaxed she found the evening enjoyable. It was nostalgic, hearing the girls singing the old songs. When they were invited to join in she found herself singing along, remembering the words effortlessly. Beside her, William sang too, his pleasant baritone blending with her soprano. The choir finished with the Skye Boat Song, and when it ended he leaned across and said, 'We make a good double act, Corrie. At least our voices seem to agree.'

She turned to look at him. Meeting the candid green eyes, she thought for the briefest of moments how surprising it was that such a plain, unattractive boy could grow into such a good-looking man, then she saw that wicked glint come into his eyes again.

'Maybe if we tried really hard we'd find we even quite liked each other,' he added.

'I think that'd be stretching optimism to the full.' She began to gather up her jacket and bag. 'I think I'd better be going now. It wouldn't look good to stay out too late—after all, this is only my second night with Sheila.' William half rose, but she shook her head. 'No, you stay. I've got the car outside.'

Out in the car park she climbed into the Rover's high driving seat and turned the ignition key. The car gave a reproachful grunt. She tried again, several times, but nothing happened. She turned the engine off. Maybe she'd flooded the carburettor. She waited, tapping her fingers against the steering wheel.

'Hello—having trouble?' To her intense annoyance William's face appeared at the car window.

'Not at all. I'm just waiting for the carburettor to clear,' she told him.

He smiled and shook his head. 'Women are always too heavy on the choke. Shift over and let me start her for you. These old cars can be a bit tricky.'

'No, thanks, I can manage perfectly,' she told him. 'Why don't you go back to your friends?'

'Mind my own business, you mean?'

She switched on the ignition again. 'Something like that.' It was meant to be a parting shot, delivered as she roared away into the sunset. But once again the engine groaned and died, ruining her exit.

William cleared his throat. 'Er—just one tiny point. . .'

'All right, go on.'

'Did you happen to notice that you're out of petrol?'

'Oh, *no*!'

To his credit he didn't laugh. 'Sheila is notoriously lax about filling up. The times Dad and I have had to rescue her!' He opened the door. 'Come on, I'll take you back to Glencoe House and I'll have the car collected in the morning.'

Corrie had no choice but to do as he said. Climbing out, she followed him across the car park and got into the passenger seat of the scarlet sports car.

'It's very good of you,' she said grudgingly.

'Not at all.'

He nosed the car out on to the road and they drove in silence for a while. The moon was just rising, hanging heavy and golden over the loch. Corrie breathed in the heather-scented air. William looked at her.

'Good to be back?' he asked.

'Yes. Even better than I'd expected it to be.'

'Glencarron is a great place to recharge the batteries,' he observed. 'To feed the starving soul, as the poet says.'

'I think my soul is reasonably well nourished, thank you.'

He pulled over to the side of the road and switched off the engine. 'Corrie, we're not going to keep up this sparring, are we? After all, we are supposed to be adults now.'

'You could have fooled me,' she told him.

He sighed. 'OK, I shouldn't have made that stupid remark about you tearing your knickers. I should have known better. But I haven't been able to do or say a thing right since, have I? And it wasn't all me, you know. You were no angel yourself.' He turned his face and bent closer, pointing to his left chek. 'See that?' There was a tiny crescent-shaped scar at the side of his nose. 'You did that.'

'*I* did?' she echoed.

'You certainly did. I think you were trying to scratch my eyes out at the time.'

'There must have been a good reason.' Suddenly the memory came back to her. She'd been eight, William twelve. She'd insisted on going fishing with him, and he'd rewarded her by putting a frog in one of her wellingtons. She remembered scratching his face now, but she also remembered that he'd pushed her into the loch for her pains.

'You gave me a soaking,' she reminded him.

'Ah, but *I've* still got the scar.'

She laughed in spite of herself. '*Touché*. Point to you, I think.'

'Tell you what—tennis is safer than fencing. Let's call it game, set and match. Better still, love all.' He leaned across and kissed her very gently on the lips. Feeling her stiffen, he drew back to study her face. 'Oh-oh, am I not even allowed a brotherly salute? You can't still be that angry with me?'

She found she was trembling and quite suddenly close to tears. 'No, William. It's just—just. . .'

'It's OK.' He started the car again. 'You don't have to tell me about it.'

She glanced at him quickly, She didn't have to tell him that the close proximity of a man—*any* man—made her think of Hugh, that even the most casual of kisses made her remember what she was trying so desperately hard to forget. She didn't have to tell him because *he had read all about it in her letter*. He knew all too well how vulnerable she was.

CHAPTER THREE

WITHIN a month of Corrie's arrival at Glencarron Sheila had settled into her new routine, but the month wasn't an easy one. For Sheila the transition from living a full, healthy life to one coping with an illness didn't come easily. Her moods swung between depressed resignation and rebellion, and those around her found life far from easy. She grumbled about the diet, saying it was boring and didn't satisfy her appetite; she complained that the exercise therapy made her limbs ache. But the daily rest period and the curtailment of her work infuriated and frustrated her more than all the rest put together.

Finally Dr Walter decided that drastic action must be taken. It was one day when he, Corrie and Sheila were sitting in the garden after lunch, trying to arrange a new work schedule. Walter had just suggested that Sheila's counselling sessions should be cut to two a week.

'If I can't work then the rest of it's a waste of time,' she burst out angrily. 'I might just as well give up!'

Dr Walter and Corrie exchanged a look. 'Sheila,' he said firmly, 'stop being so damned obstructive and do as you're told. If you don't you'll end up as a chronic invalid.'

Her mouth tightened. 'Then stop treating me like a child,' she said petulantly.

'If you stopped *behaving* like a child—and a spoilt

one at that—I might start treating you differently,'
Walter told her sternly. 'Just stop and think a minute.
Would you ever have tolerated this kind of behaviour
from your pupils in the old days? And what would
you tell a patient who came for advice and then
wouldn't take it?'

Corrie held her breath. She'd never heard anyone
speak to Sheila Fraser like that before. But to her
surprise Sheila's expression dissolved, to be replaced
by a distinctly hangdog look.

'Oh, all right, you bully,' she sighed. 'I suppose
I've got to eat like a rabbit, bend and stretch like a
demented muscle-man and then lie about like a sloth
all afternoon. It's undignified and ridiculous, but if
that's what it takes, then I suppose it's what I'm
condemned to.'

'*And* you should do it with a good grace,' said
Walter, pressing his point. 'If you do it grudgingly,
you might as well not bother. For heaven's sake,
Sheila, don't you *want* to help yourself?'

'I don't want to be *ill*,' she said, her anger recharg-
ing itself.

'Illness is a state of mind,' Corrie put in. 'Your
condition won't go away, but it needn't be an illness
unless you let it. By turning your back on it you're
letting it win.'

'Corrie's right,' said Walter. 'Face it and fight it,
Sheila—with all the weapons you're being offered.
Good practical ones. Burying your head in the sand
just makes you blind—can't you understand that?'

Sheila sighed. 'I'm outnumbered,' she said. 'It isn't
fair. You, Walter; Corrie and William—even Kathy.'

'We're on your side,' Corrie said quietly. 'You're

the only one on the side of MS. You're letting it beat you.'

Sheila stood up. 'I'm going up to have my rest,' she said.

'Are you all right?' Walter was on his feet immediately, but Sheila shook off the arm he offered.

'Of course I'm all right, you fussy little man,' she said. 'It's what you want, isn't it? I'm "doing as I'm told". Aren't you ever satisfied?' She walked off towards the house with as much dignity as she could muster. When she was out of earshot Corrie looked at the doctor.

'Oh, dear! Is she upset?'

He smiled and shook his head. 'That's Sheila's way of giving in,' he told her. 'She'll never admit it, of course, but she's seen the sense in what we've told her all right. Somehow I don't think we'll have any more trouble from her.'

And he was right. Sheila got up from her rest in a completely different frame of mind. She enjoyed the evening meal that Corrie prepared for her, and even admitted how much better she was beginning to feel. After they had cleared the meal away Corrie asked her if she wanted to watch the television, but Sheila shook her head.

'I don't know why I bother with the thing,' she said. 'Because of Craecuillin the signal is so bad we get a poor reception. And when the weather's good it's even worse—like peering through a snowstorm.'

'When the weather's good at Glencarron, who wants to watch television anyway?' smiled Corrie. 'Shall we sit in the garden for a while?'

'We might as well make the most if it,' Sheila

chuckled. 'Another couple of months and the midges will be out in full force.'

Sitting on the little wooden seat under the sitting-room window, with the intoxicating scent of honey-suckle filling the air, Sheila sighed.

'It's so peaceful, isn't it? I'm so lucky to live here.' She glanced at Corrie. 'I'm sorry about this afternoon, my dear.'

'Nothing to apologise for. Anger's better than complacency, when all's said and done. It just needs channelling in the right direction.'

Sheila looked at her. 'Everything you say makes such good sense. You know, since you've been here you've surprised me more than once with your level-headed view of life,' she said. 'I'm sure you could help with the counselling sessions. If you did we wouldn't have to cut them down. It seems such a shame when so many people need help.'

'I'm surprised that there are so many needing help here in a peaceful place like Glencarron,' Corrie remarked.

'Life's pressures find their way into even the most idyllic corners.' There was a pause, then Sheila asked, 'Have *you* found peace here?'

Corrie looked up at her in surprise. 'I came here to work with you.'

'And a little because you were. . .' Sheila put her head on one side. 'Would *running away* sound too strong?'

Corrie sighed. 'No, not really, though I didn't have much choice'

'A man?'

She nodded. 'What else would have made me throw up my job. . .?'

'And go to the back of beyond to look after a cantankerous old woman?' Sheila chuckled heartily at her own ending of Corrie's sentence, waving away the protestation it aroused. 'No, don't deny it—that's what you did. And you certainly deserve better than what you've had to put up with these last weeks. But I promise that from now on I'm turning over a new leaf. I'm going to beat this wretched thing if it's the last thing. . .' She stopped short. 'No, the *first* thing I do.'

Corrie smiled. 'Good for you! That's the spirit. And as for what I've had to put up with, we'll forget that. Nothing worthwhile comes easily, after all.'

'Well, I'm glad you think I'm worthwhile and not a lost cause.' Sheila settled a cushion more comfortably into the small of her back and looked thoughtfully at her. 'Right, so are you going to tell me your real reason for coming here?'

'Well, to begin with, it wasn't as you said,' Corrie began. 'I wanted to get away, it's true, but when I saw the advertisement Uncle Walt put in the nursing journal it was like a dream come true. To be able to come home and look after you was more than I could have hoped for.'

'Did he hurt you very badly?' Sheila asked softly.

'Uncle Walt didn't tell you, then?'

Sheila looked surprised. 'He most certainly didn't! You must know him better than that. Walter would never betray a confidence.'

'OK, but I wouldn't have minded,' said Corrie. 'I

wrote and told him because it could have made a
difference to your employing me.'

'Well, he must have used his own judgement.'
Sheila smiled. 'And he knows I trust that.'

'Well, as you've guessed, I—fell in love,' Corrie
began haltingly, 'with a consultant surgeon I worked
with. He was brilliant and handsome and
charismatic.'

'And married?' Sheila cocked an eyebrow at her.

Corrie sighed. 'Yes—and married. But I didn't
know that until it was too late. He said he was going
to ask his wife for a divorce.'

'In other words, he strung you along.'

'I suppose he did. But I could have stood that. I
could have put up with the waiting, the let-downs,
the long empty hours when he couldn't see me. He
said we'd be together eventually, you see. He said he
loved me, that I was—all that he'd ever wanted. . .'
Her voice trailed off as she fought down the lump that
threatened to close her throat. 'It was the deceit I
couldn't take.'

'Didn't you guess that he might be deceitful?' Sheila
said gently. 'After all, he was deceiving his wife,
wasn't he?'

'I suppose I closed my eyes to that. He said the
marriage was over, you see—that it had been for
years. He told me his wife was cold, that she didn't
care about him. He said she took no pride in their
home or her appearance—that the marriage had
scarcely been consummated.'

'And. . .?'

'And then I found out that they had three teenage
children that he'd never mentioned,' Corrie said

bitterly. 'I saw him with them all at an open day at
the hospital. I'd said I was going on holiday with a
friend, but at the last minute I hadn't gone—couldn't
tear myself away. I thought I'd go to the open day
and surprise him. He was there with his wife and
family. They all looked so happy together. She—his
wife—was one of the most beautiful, elegant women
I've ever seen. She wasn't the way he'd described her
at all.'

'Oh, my dear!'

'But that wasn't all. I found out later that her father
was a very eminent surgeon—a knight. Obviously
he'd have been a great help to Hugh's career. I
couldn't see him divorcing his wife and throwing
away all his career prospects just like that. I knew
then that I'd been no more than a—pleasant diver-
sion for him.'

'Did you see him again?' asked Sheila.

Corrie nodded, wincing at the memory. 'He took it
all as a matter of course. He said I was bound to find
out one day. He said we'd had a marvellous time and
that he'd always remember me.'

'Didn't he offer you any consolation at all?' Sheila
asked.

'Oh, yes. Just as he was leaving he looked at me
and said, "Don't be unhappy about it, Corrie. You're
probably better off without me. Chances are I'd have
deceived you too before long."'

Sheila drew her breath in sharply. 'There's a word
for men like that!'

Corrie shivered. 'I think we should go indoors now.
Can't have you catching cold.'

'Before we do there's something I want to ask you.

Will you take some counselling sessions for me?' asked Sheila.

Corrie pulled a face. 'After what I've just told you? Don't you think I'm too stupid and näive?'

'I think you've learned a valuable lesson in living, one you won't forget.' Sheila leaned forward. 'You told me that this—illne—this *condition* of mine would help me to help others. That applies to you too, doesn't it?'

'Well, of course if a suitable case comes along—and if you really think I can help. . .'

'I do,' Sheila smiled.

'Well, all right, then, I'll give it a try.'

The 'suitable case' came for Corrie sooner than she'd imagined it would. The following day William called in to give Sheila her monthly check. Examining her, he found her much improved.

'It's working, Sheila,' he told her with a smile. 'You're co-operating and it's all coming together nicely. I think we can safely say that you can begin your counselling again next week. I'm sure that'll please you.'

'It does,' Sheila told him with a smile. 'Even a curtailed schedule is better than nothing. Corrie has said she'll help too.'

William looked at her thoughtfully. 'That's interesting. As a matter of fact, I do have a case that you might help with, Corrie. Maybe we could talk about it.'

'Right, I'm ready,' said Corrie.

'Not now, I'm too pushed for time.' Wiliam looked

at his watch. 'How about a drive out somewhere this evening? Maybe a bite to eat?'

Corrie looked doubtfully at Sheila, but the older woman nodded encouragingly.

'Just what you need, my dear. You have only been out once since you came here. You could do with a break.'

'But what about you?'

'For heaven's sake, how do you think I managed before you came?' Sheila smiled at William. 'Call for her—I'll see that she's ready. And be sure and take her somewhere nice. She deserves it.'

'Right, you're on,' he grinned triumphantly. 'Eight o'clock. Be sure and wear something stunning. I'll look forward to—er—telling you about this case.' The wicked teasing glint was back in his eyes again, but Corrie ignored it as she walked with him to his car.

'I'll look forward to *hearing about the case* too,' she said.

He arrived just as Sheila's grandfather clock was striking the hour. Walking into the house in his customary casual manner, he asked Sheila, 'Well, is she ready?'

'I'm sure she is. Just call up the stairs for her, will you?'

Going into the hall, William shouted up the stairs, 'Corrie, I'm here! Don't you know it's bad manners to keep a man waiting?'

In the doorway of her room Corrie ground her teeth with irritation. For some reason she didn't really understand she'd taken a lot of trouble with her appearance. She wore a silky flame-coloured dress that she'd bought recently for a friend's engagement party. With it she wore black patent shoes and carried a small purse to match. When she reached the top of the stairs she found him standing at the bottom, looking up at her. He gave a long, low whistle.

'Phew—when I said stunning I didn't think you'd take me at my word! Glencarron will wonder what's hit it!'

Corrie coloured. 'If you think it's too much. . .'

'No, not at all. I was only teasing. Anyway, we're giving Glencarron a miss this evening. I've booked a table for us at a little place I know. It's a drive out from here.'

'You mean you're not likely to be seen by anyone you know, so it'll be all right.'

William shook his head. 'Ah—touchy as ever! Oh, come away down, woman. You look just fine. I'll be proud to be seen with you.'

It was a fine evening, but William had put up the car's soft top. 'I know what you girls are,' he explained. 'Forever fussing about your hair.'

'You often take girls out in the car, then?' she asked.

'Well, of course.' He grinned wickedly at her. 'What's the use of a sports car without a pretty girl to put in the passenger seat? It's a must.'

'And tonight I'm filling that position. Lucky, *lucky* me!'

He glanced at her. 'You should watch that tongue. You're beginning to sound like an embittered woman.'

She swung round to face him. 'And what does that mean?'

'What it says,' he told her calmly. 'Since you went away you seem to have developed the most unattractive waspishness. I know we used to fight as kids, but this is different. It's almost as though you're afraid of me getting the better of you—getting your punches in first, when all I really want is for us to be friends. I thought we'd called a truce.'

'Of course we have,' she conceded. 'Sorry.'

'Just wait till you see where I'm taking you. Maybe it'll make up. Just for this evening we're going to be tourists.'

They drove for about an hour, through some of the most spectacular scenery in Scotland, ending up on the outskirts of Fort William. The Croft was a quiet restaurant where the waitresses wore tartan dresses and there was heather on all the tables. William looked slightly apologetic as they were shown to their table.

'I promise you the food is excellent, in spite of the naff décor,' he told her. 'And before you accuse me of patronising you. . .'

She laughed. 'I wasn't going to.'

'Great. We're making progress.'

Corrie found that he was right, the food was good. They ate fresh, locally caught salmon with the tenderest of vegetables, and the sweet trolley was a delight of calorie-laden succulence. Over the meal William told her a little about his years at university and later at medical school, making her laugh at some of his earlier experiences, with which she could identify from her own training.

'We seem to have missed each other's adolescence,' he said. 'I always asked after you when I came home, but I always seemed to have just missed you.'

'Probably just as well,' Corrie remarked wryly.

'Would you be surprised to learn that I was disappointed?' he asked.

She smiled. 'I would.'

'It's true. I was curious about you. I wondered how you'd turned out—what kind of woman you'd grown into.'

'And now you know that I'm not much different from the horrid little girl you loathed so much all those years ago.'

For a moment he was silent, then he said, 'I didn't really loathe you, Corrie.'

She smiled. 'No? You could have fooled me.'

'I wonder if you'd believe me if I told you the truth?'

'I might—if you think I could stand the shock.'

'Careful—you're being waspish again,' he warned.

'Sorry. Go on, I'm curious. What *is* the truth of it?' asked Corrie.

'I was jealous.'

She stared at him. '*Jealous*—of me? I don't believe it!'

'There, I said you wouldn't. It's true. I knew Dad had always wanted a little daughter, and my mother died giving birth to a baby girl. Maybe you never knew that.'

'No, I didn't.'

'The baby died with her. Naturally he was shattered. For a long time he was so preoccupied he hardly seemed to notice I was there. In an odd way I felt he blamed me—that it should have been me he lost. Later, when your father came to join the practice, and brought you with him, I could see that Dad was taken with you. He adored you when you were a little girl, and it hurt. I resented you bitterly.'

She found herself touched at his confession and reached out to touch his hand. 'William, I had no idea.'

He grinned suddenly. 'How I hated you, with your clean white ankle socks and your sunny smile! I was convinced you were playing up to Dad. I was just an ugly great gangling lad, but *you*—you could twist those two men around your little finger, with your dainty ways and those big brown eyes of yours.'

'But I *didn't*!' she protested. 'I was totally unaware of all this. I wasn't in the least devious, William.' She leaned across the table. 'If we're exchanging confidences, I'll tell *you* something now. All I really wanted was to be able to climb trees and swim and fish like you. I wanted great big dirty knees just like yours and to be allowed to get filthy. You were my hero really— even though you were rotten to me most of the time. You did some terrible things to me in those days.'

The next moment they were both laughing.

'I can't say there was much evidence of my being your hero,' William said with feeling. 'My goodness, though, but you had a temper! You could pack a pretty hefty punch too, in spite of those innocent, fragile looks. More than once you knocked the wind out of me. You were unscrupulous too. You played dirty. You'd do anything—scratch—bite, no holds barred. . .' He looked at her speculatively. 'I've an idea you still can hit hard.'

'One more allusion to my big brown eyes and innocent fragile looks and you could find out,' she warned him.

'So—what happened down there in London?' he asked as they reached the end of the meal.

Corrie looked up at him sharply. 'What do you mean, what happened?'

'Something must have happened to make you throw up the post of theatre sister and come back here to a temporary job with Sheila.'

She thought of her letter to Dr Walter. Was he trying to lead her into telling him what he already knew?

'I wanted a change,' she said evasively. 'London is fine. For the first few years it's exciting and challenging. But after a while one feels the need to get away from it all—recharge the batteries, if you like.'

'You could have moved to a smaller town,' he said. 'Some provincial hospital would have snapped you up, especially after the eminent surgeons you'd worked with.'

Eminent surgeons; was that another hint? She glanced at him, but his face gave nothing away. 'Are you telling me I'm wasting my time?'

'Not at all. Far be it from me to tell you anything. You know your own business best.' He paused, then, 'Corrie, there's nothing wrong, is there?'

'Why do you ask?' She heard the defensive snap in her voice and bit her lip.

He shrugged. 'It's just that there's a certain wistful look in your eyes sometimes.'

'Really?' She was well and truly on her guard now. 'I might as well ask you the same questions, William.

Why should *you* bury yourself up here in a small Highland town when you could be working in a city and getting so much more experience?'

He bridled slightly. 'If there has to be a reason, then I suppose I wanted to please Dad,' he said. 'He's never said so, but I knew it was his dream that I should take over from him one day. Anyway, I happen to like it here. It's my home.'

'How simple life is for some people,' Corrie sighed.

'Are you being sarcastic, or do I detect a note of bitterness?'

'Neither,' she said, meeting his eyes sincerely. 'I meant it, William. I envy you, I really do.' She drank the last of her coffee and looked at him. 'So tell me about this case you think I might be able to help with.'

He looked around. 'I'll just get the bill first and we'll talk in the car. I wouldn't like to be overheard.'

Out in the car park the light was just beginning to fade. As they climbed into the car William said, 'We'll drive up to the Commando Memorial, shall we? It'll be quiet there.'

It was years since Corrie had seen the Commando Memorial that stood just above Fort William at the foot of the hills where the Commandos had trained during the war. William parked the car and they got out to look up at the movingly beautiful faces of the four soldiers depicted there. Tears came to Corrie's eyes.

'It's so beautiful,' she said. 'Their faces say it all, don't they? It has strength and dignity, and a terrible vulnerability too. It always makes me want to cry.'

William's arm encircled her shoulders and pulled

her close to his side. 'It's certainly a fitting memorial,' he agreed.

She looked up at him. 'You were going to tell me about this case you think I could help with.'

'Yes.' He looked thoughtful as they walked slowly back to the car. 'The young woman in question is about your age. She did well at school and I believe she had plans to study law. But her mother died when she was eighteen, leaving her to care for an invalid father. Recently she's been coming to me with all kinds of nebulous symptoms—asking for tranquillisers.'

'Looking after an elderly relative can be trying for a young person,' Corrie said. 'Is there any chance of her having a break?'

William shook his head. 'Possibly, but I happen to think there's more to it than that.' He turned to her. 'I can tell you this, Corrie, because I haven't revealed the patient's name as yet. When she first came to me I had to ask if she was taking any other form of medication before prescribing tablets.'

'Of course.'

'And I discovered she was taking a contraceptive pill.'

'One that you hadn't prescribed, you mean?' she queried.

'Exactly. It appears she'd been all the way to Inverness to a family planning clinic.'

'So—she was too embarrassed to come to you for it.'

He shook his head. 'For whatever purpose she needed it, it isn't making her happy. I've watched the girl go downhill rapidly over the past two months. I carried out a full routine examination and could find nothing physically wrong with her. But if something isn't done soon she'll be into a nervous breakdown.'

'Do you think she's putting off marriage because of her father?' asked Corrie.

'No. I happen to think marriage is out of the question.'

'Why?'

'I get the feeling that whoever the man is, he isn't free to marry her,' William explained.

'What makes you think that?'

'Just a hunch. She wouldn't be eating her heart out like this over a mere postponement.'

There was a pause during which Corrie felt the familiar ice-cold void open up inside her again. 'You mean you think the man might already be married?' She had to force herself to say it.

'Something along those lines.'

For a long moment Corrie paused. 'William, why do you think I'm the person to tackle this?' she asked at last.

'I told you—she's your age. I'm not suggesting that you have the answer—that's not what counselling is about. It's largely just a question of listening. Sometimes it helps to talk to a sympathetic person. I think you and she would like each other.' He was looking straight at her and she made herself meet his eyes.,

'And you just happen to know that *I* was recently in love with a man who was married?'

The expression in his eyes changed to one of shock. 'I haven't the faintest idea what you're talking about.'

'No?'

'*No*, damn it.' He frowned and ran a hand through his hair. 'Look, Corrie, if I'd known a thing like that do you really think I'd have been so insensitive as to. . .' He broke off, peering into her eyes. 'You *do*, don't you? You really believe I'd pull a stroke like that on you? How could I possibly have known a thing like that, anyway?'

'The letter I—wrote to your father—the one you told me you'd passed on. I thought it was only fair to tell him my reason for applying for the job. I didn't know he'd retired, so I addressed it to Doctor W. Forbes, care of the surgery.'

'And you thought I would have *read* it before giving it to him?'

'You might have thought—naturally—that it was for you,' she pointed out.

'Well, I didn't. He started the car. 'As soon as I saw the signature I passed it straight to Dad. A lot of letters still come to the surgery for him. It wasn't unusual.'

For several minutes Corrie sat silently in her seat beside him. She felt ashamed now of what she'd accused him of. William and she were adults now. It really was time she forgot their childhood quarrels. It was she who was being small-minded and petty, not him. At last she turned to him and said quietly, 'William, I'm sorry, I think my recent—problem must have warped my mind a little.'

'Don't mention it. And don't think I don't know how it feels, Corrie. I *do*.' His profile, silhouetted against the car window in the fading light, looked gaunt and uncompromising. He didn't look at her but stared straight ahead as he drove. Obviously he had no intention of expanding on his remark.

Neither of them spoke again for the remainder of

the journey. To Corrie it seemed endless. She searched her mind for something to say to break the ice, but her mind seemed to have gone completely blank. Finally William slowed to take the sharp bend that led on to the track and the car bumped over the uneven ground until it came to a halt at the foot of the steps to Glencoe House. Corrie turned to him.

'Thank you for a lovely evening,' she said.

He laughed shortly. 'The polite, well brought up little girl to the end!'

'Please, don't. I've said I'm sorry,' she said quietly. 'And, William, I *will* see the patient you were talking about. Whatever—whatever instinct told you I'd be sympathetic was right.'

He turned to look at her at last, and this time his expression was softer. 'You're sure? It won't be too traumatic?'

'No, I won't let it be. And yes, I'm sure.'

'Right. Thanks. Of course, I don't know if she'll agree to counselling yet,' he added. 'But I'll make the suggestion to her and give you a ring if she agrees.'

'Right. I'll wait to hear from you.' She got out of the car and stood on the steps, watching as he turned the car and drove back along the track to climb on to the road again. She'd learned things about William this evening that she'd never known before. He had his vulnerable side too—but the masculine pride was as strong as ever. She'd dented that pride tonight. Years ago, in their feuding days, that would have given her a feeling of triumph, but now she felt that her own dignity was the casualty. She'd made a fool of herself. And she'd needlessly given away her secret into the bargain.

CHAPTER FOUR

SHEILA had wakened in a depressed mood. Over breakfast Corrie tried to cheer her.

'Christie is coming today. You always enjoy seeing her, don't you?'

'I suppose so.' Sheila sighed. 'Corrie, I suppose I should tell you. For the past two days I've been getting double vision.'

'Why didn't you tell me?'

Sheila shrugged. 'I didn't want to bother you.'

'You mean you thought it would go away if you ignored it. Sheila, what do you think I'm here for?' sighed Corrie.

'I know, I know. Don't scold me.'

'Maybe you've been trying to do too much,' Corrie said. 'It could just be tiredness. Do you want me to ask William to look in?'

'No. He's due tomorrow anyway. It might have gone by then.'

Corrie nodded. 'Well, we'll see what Christie thinks when she arrives.'

But Christie had a more positive suggestion. 'I know a lady who's a reflexologist,' she said. 'She works with your feet and claims she can tell what's wrong just by looking at them. She's had particularly good results with visual problems. Will you try her, Sheila?'

Sheila looked sceptical. 'Cure my double vision by massaging my *feet*? Whatever next?'

'I promise you it does work,' Christie assured her. 'And if it doesn't it can't hurt you, can it?'

'What will William say?' Sheila asked. 'I don't want to upset him.'

'Unlike some doctors, William has an open mind as far as fringe medicine is concerned,' Christie told her.

She examined Sheila and put her through her exercise routine. Afterwards she took Corrie to one side. 'Has she been doing the exercises regularly?' she asked.

'Every day. Why?'

'Her legs aren't responding as well as they might.'

Corrie looked thoughtful. 'She does complain that the leg exercises make her muscles ache,' she said.

Christie shook her head. 'The weaker her legs get the less she's likely to use them, and it's a vicious circle. Do you think she'd treat herself to an exercise cycle?'

'I don't know. It might not be the time to ask her—she's a bit depressed today,' Corrie explained.

'Well, bear it in mind, and bring up the subject when you feel the time is right. She could do with something to keep her hands supple too. Does she have any hobbies? Needlework might be a good one. Maybe it would keep the depression at bay too.'

'I'll talk to her,' Corrie promised.

'And make sure she rests enough. Don't let her do too much counselling.'

Corrie laughed. 'A tall order, but I'll try.'

Over coffee Christie suggested to Sheila that she might like to join one of the groups for the disabled.

'Sometimes it's useful to swap ideas and compare notes with others in a similar situation,' she said. But Sheila shook her head firmly.

'That would only depress me,' she said. 'I'd really feel crippled if I joined one of those. It would feel like giving in.'

'Sheila,' Christie said gently, 'any kind of disablement is basically the same, from MS to alcoholism. One can't be helped until one has admitted to it. It's nothing to be ashamed of.'

Sheila stood up and straightened her back with determination. 'Thank you for comparing me with an alcoholic, Christie,' she said coldly. 'If you'll excuse me, I have some notes to look at. I'll be in my study if either of you needs me.'

As the door closed behind her Christie looked at Corrie and winced. 'Ouch! I put both feet in it that time!'

'It's just her mood. She'll get over it,' Corrie told her. 'Frankly, on days like this I think her counselling session does more good than anything else. It helps her forget her own troubles.'

'Well, William knows best about that, I suppose. If he says she can work, it must be all right.' Christie looked at her watch. 'I'd better get going, I suppose.' As Corrie was walking out to the car with her she said, 'Oh, by the way, I hear you and William have been dining together?'

'News travels fast!' laughed Corrie.

'You must have forgotten that you can't keep a secret long in Glencarron,' Christie smiled. 'Especially one concerning affairs of the heart.'

'Affairs of the heart? If that's what people think

about William and me they'll be disappointed,' said Corrie. 'Our dinner was pleasant, but it was purely professional.'

'Really? You'd have a job convincing the folk of Glencarron of that,' Christie laughed as she climbed into her car.

'I'm not treading on your toes by any chance, am I?' asked Corrie, bending down to look in at the window.

Christie paused in the act of fastening her seat belt. 'Toes? *My* toes? Good heavens, no!'

'I just wondered. You and William used to like each other quite a lot, didn't you?' Corrie was thinking of William's enigmatic remark, *Don't think I don't know how it feels, Corrie. I do.*

Christie smiled. 'Corrie, I do believe you're still smarting over that school dance all those years ago! William only asked me to the dance that time to annoy you, surely you know that?'

Corrie blushed. She'd rather hoped that that particular embarrassing situation would have been forgotten by all concerned. 'No—I just had the idea that you and he. . .'

'I think Peter might have something to say about that,' Christie said as she started the engine.

'Peter? The young man you were with at the Gordon Arms that evening?'

'That's right. We've been going out together for almost a year now.' Christie paused. 'William did have a rather special girlfriend while he was doing his pre-reg stint, I believe. He brought her home once to meet his father. I heard she was about to be divorced. Then it seems the ex-husband came back and they

decided to get together again.' She engaged first gear
and let off the handbrake. 'I must go now, Corrie.
'Bye, see you soon.'

Corrie walked slowly back up the steps. So that was
what Wiliam had meant when he said he understood
how it felt. She found herself slightly surprised at her
own curiosity about the matter and pulled herself up
sharply. After all, it didn't matter to her at all, did it?
It was really none of her business.

Sheila's mood didn't improve, and when William
called early next morning on his way to the surgery
she was still in bed. Corrie mentioned her depression
to him.

'She's very down at the moment. She confessed to
me yesterday that she's been having double vision.
Christie suggested reflexology. Are you in favour?'

He nodded. 'Anything that helps is fine as far as
I'm concerned.'

'Christie also suggested joining one of the groups
for disabled people.'

William laughed. 'Don't tell me—I can guess.'

'You're right, I'm afraid. William, has Sheila ever
had a hobby? Apart from her work, I mean?'

He frowned. 'Not that I know of. Dad would be the
one to ask.'

'I'll mention it to him when he comes for this
afternoon's counselling session,' said Corrie.

'That brings me to what I was going to tell you,'
William said. 'The girl I mentioned to you the other
evening—she's agreed to see you. Is this afternoon all
right?'

'Yes, of course.'

'I said I'd make the appointment for her. I thought if I left it to her to telephone she'd probably chicken out. Her name is Kirsty, by the way.'

'Fine. Thanks,' Corrie said.

'And she'll be here at two-thirty. A neighbour will sit with her father for an hour. Is that all right?'

Corrie laughed. 'It'll have to be, won't it?'

He frowned. 'I'm not bulldozing you into it, am I?'

'No. My only concern is that I might not be of any help to the girl.'

'I'm sure you will. It's basically just listening,' he said. 'More than anything else, Kirsty needs a friendly ear to pour her troubles into; someone who won't make judgements.' He smiled. 'Now, shall we go up and see Sheila?'

Sheila was sitting up in bed, her breakfast tray in front of her, the food on it barely touched. William sat on the edge of the bed and looked at it.

'What's all this? Not hungry?' He took a slice of crispbread from the toast rack and began to spread it. 'Hope you don't mind. I was up half the night at a confinement and I overslept this morning. I didn't have time for any breakfast.'

'What you need, William Forbes, is a good wife to look after you.' Sheila watched him munch the crispbread. 'That stuff is no good for a strapping young man like you. If you ask me, it's only fit for hamsters. As for that poly-whatsitsname spread. . .' she raised her eyes to the ceiling, 'words fail me!'

William paused to look at her. 'Tastes fine to me. Healthy too.' He cocked an eyebrow at her. 'Well, how are you? Anything to tell me?'

Sheila glanced at Corrie. 'Do we have to keep up

this charade? Do I have to pretend that Corrie hasn't reported to you that I'm as grouchy as hell—finding fault with everything and being thoroughly bloody-minded?'

'Is that how you seem to *you*, Sheila?' William asked gravely. 'Corrie certainly hasn't said so. She did say you seemed a bit down, though. Why do you think that is?'

Sheila looked a little ashamed. 'Oh, I suppose I'm just sorry for myself, if the truth were known,' she said. 'And Christie lumping me along with alcoholics yesterday didn't help.'

William laughed. 'She told me about that. Hardly the soul of tact, is she? She means well, though. I hear she suggested joining a disabled group. That's not a bad idea. There's an organisation called ARMS—it stands for Action for Research into MS. I could find out for you where the nearest group meets, if you like.'

'No, thanks.'

He squeezed her hand. 'Sheila, there are a lot of MS sufferers, you know, from all walks of life. Some are young men with families to provide for. They have to find a way to keep going. There are young mothers with children to care for, old people with no money, youngsters without parents. Joining a group shows you that there's always someone worse off than you are. Sometimes you can even help, and you know that always makes you feel better, because you're a naturally generous person.'

'Oh, William, I'm not generous. I'm a selfish, thoughtless old woman.' Tears began to trickle down Sheila's cheeks, and William did nothing to stop them. Instead he pulled a tissue from the box by the bed and pushed it into her hand.

'That's right, have a good cry,' he said gently. 'You bottle things up far too much, you know. Letting go is probably just what you need. At least it's positive.' He patted her shoulder. 'Look, I'll come in again tomorrow. If you feel like it why not rest today?'

She sniffed, dabbing her eyes, recovering quickly. 'No, I want to take my counselling session this afternoon. Walter's coming to lunch too. I must get up.'

'Right, then, I'll see you tomorrow.' Downstairs in the hall William turned to Corrie. 'Depression is part of MS,' he said. 'But fatigue and low blood sugar only make matters worse, so don't let her get away with not eating. And make sure she rests enough.' He looked thoughtful. 'That hobby idea is a good one. See if you can work the conversation round to it at lunch. I'll put in a word with Dad.'

She walked out to the car with him, quietly impressed at his perception and understanding of Sheila's nature as well as her illness, and relieved too that he appeared to bear her no grudge for her unjust accusation.

'Thanks for calling, William,' she said. 'I'm sure you've helped.'

He turned to face her. 'How about you, Corrie— are you all right?'

'Of course. Why do you ask?'

'You're looking a little pale.'

'I'm fine, thank you,' she assured him.

'Right then, see you tomorrow. Um. . .' He hesitated, one hand on the car door handle.

'What?'

'I was wondering—there's a dance at the Gordon Arms next week. Would you like to go?'

'I'm sure there are a dozen other girls just lining up to go with you.' She was aware of how ungracious her words sounded, but William only laughed.

'Naturally—dozens, I dare say, but I'm asking you, so they'll just have to eat their hearts out.'

'Wouldn't Christie go with you this time?' she queried.

The barb failed to find its mark. 'No, worse luck.' He shook his head regretfully. 'She's going out with this Peter bloke she's so taken with.' He grinned. 'No accounting for taste, is there? Still. . .' he got into the car and smiled up at her. '. . .her loss could be your gain. How about it?'

Corrie smiled in spite of herself. 'You're so modest, Dr Forbes,' she said. 'I'll let you know about the dance.' She turned towards the house.

'Don't leave it too long,' he called to her. 'You know how scarce eligible men are in Glencarron!' She pretended not to hear.

As it happened, there was no need for anyone to mention a hobby for Sheila. She emerged looking much more cheerful about an hour after William's visit. She had dressed in her favourite heather-coloured tweed skirt and a sweater of sky blue that brought out the colour of her eyes. Corrie found her rummaging in the cupboard under the stairs.

'Anything I can help with?' she asked.

'I'm looking for my old sketching things,' came the muffled reply. 'I used to have some watercolour paints too. I looked out of the window this morning, lying up there in bed, and I suddenly thought how mad it is not to take it up again. After all, I've plenty of time now. . . Ah, *here* they are,' she said triumphantly, backing out of the cupboard clutching a cardboard box. 'I do hope they haven't all dried up.'

Corrie smiled at the flushed face and sparkling blue eyes. 'You look much better,' she said.

'I feel it.' Sheila pushed back a stray lock of hair and put the box down on the hall table. 'Promise me something, Corrie.'

'Of course—anything.'

'If ever I get like that again, kick me where it hurts most,' she said. 'Now, let's see what we have in here.' She picked up the box and carried it into the sitting-room. 'Do you know, I'm quite looking forward to having a go at painting Craecuillin again. Maybe I'll even manage not to make it look like a Christmas pudding this time!'

Lunch with Dr Walter seemed to cheer Sheila even more. In fact, he seemed quite surprised to find her so cheerful, William having warned him earlier of her depressed mood. He mentioned it to Corrie after the meal, when Sheila had gone to the kitchen to fetch the coffee.

'William said Sheila was a bit down, but she seems fine. I dare say that's all due to you.'

'Not at all—it was William,' Corrie told him. 'He talked to her and it seems to have done the trick. She's even been looking out her paints and talking of taking it up again.'

Dr Walter smiled. 'William has a way with him,'

he said with a hint of pride. 'He has an instinct for saying just the right thing.'

Corrie paused. 'I'm afraid I was rather unfair to him a few evenings ago,' she confessed. 'The letter I wrote to you about my real reason for giving up my job—the one I addressed to the surgery—because of a chance remark he made I assumed that he must have opened and read it.'

'Oh, dear!' Dr Walter sighed. 'Whatever could he have said to give you that impression?'

'It was something about relationships with people who are married,' said Corrie, unwilling to relate too much of the conversation. 'I thought he was hinting.' Dr Walter nodded understandingly.

'Ah, he'd have been trying to tell you about Fiona.'

'Fiona?'

'Yes. William met her when he was a houseman in Edinburgh. She was a physiotherapist. I wondered at the time whether he was in love with her. Anyway, it was serious enough for him to bring her home one weekend.'

'I see. And it—didn't work out?'

Dr Walter shook his head. 'She was married—well, separated. And she decided in the end to patch up her marriage. I'd like to kid myself that William came back to Glencarron because of me, but I sometimes wonder if it was just to lick his wounds that he came back.' He smiled at her a little wistfully. 'How about you, Corrie? Are you getting over your own unhappiness now? Has the old place worked its magic for you?'

She smiled at him. 'I'm fine, thanks, Uncle Walt. How could I not be with friends like you around me?'

But hearing about William's unhappy affair had brought back memories of her own—aroused painful feelings. It was different for a man, she told herself. They were more resilient, less vulnerable. William seemed to have escaped unscathed. Hugh's face suddenly filled her mind and refused to leave. She was grateful that she'd be busy this afternoon.

Dr Walter took his counselling sessions in the sitting-room at Glencoe House, while Sheila conducted hers in her small study at the other end of the ground floor. Corrie was to receive Kirsty in her own sitting-room upstairs. As two-thirty approached she watched for her from the window, and a little after the half-hour she saw a girl in a blue dress cycling down the track by the loch, her long fair hair flying in the wind. She went out to meet her.

At the bottom of the steps the girl got off her bike. Corrie smiled and held out her hand.

'Kirsty? Hello. I'm Corinne Ashley.'

The girl smiled shyly. 'It's good of you to see me like this.'

'Not at all. Would you like to come in? My place is upstairs. We'll go round to the back.'

In the pleasant little sitting-room Corrie had the kettle plugged in ready. 'I expect you'd like a cup of tea after your bike ride?'

The girl nodded. 'Thank you.'

As Corrie made the tea she noticed how edgy the girl was and wondered what she could do to put her at her ease. As she put the tray down on the coffee table between them she said, 'Look, Kirsty, this is very informal. If you feel like talking, please do, but if you've changed your mind, it doesn't matter a bit.'

'I wouldn't want you to think I was wasting your time,' Kirsty told her.

'Of course I wouldn't feel like that. Maybe it'll do you good just to get out and meet someone new. Have a change of scene.' Corrie poured the tea and offered Kirsty a biscuit. The girl shook her head, sipping her tea thoughtfully, but she looked a little more relaxed.

They talked of Glencarron, and Corrie discovered that the other girl was a year older than she and had gone to school in Inverness.

'I was wondering how I came to miss you,' she said. 'Tell me about your father.'

Kirsty put her cup down on the table. 'He has Parkinson's disease,' she said. 'As I expect you know, there's nothing much to be done about it. He relies on me, especially since Mum died. I couldn't leave him.'

'It's hard on you,' Corrie agreed.

Kirsty lifted her shoulders helplessly.

'Do you get help at all?' asked Corrie.

'A home help twice a week. And the district nurse to assist with bathing and so on.'

'What about a holiday—a break?'

'Oh, yes. Dad goes into hospital every so often so that I can get a rest. I don't go away, though.' Kirsty smiled wistfully. 'It isn't much fun on your own, is it?'

'Is there no friend you could go with?'

Kirsty paused, a hesitant expression crossing her face, then she shook her head. 'The girl friends I used to have are mostly married now, and even those that aren't, I've lost touch with. When you can't go out to socialise you tend to lose touch.'

'And there's no boyfriend?' The girl shrugged again, and Corrie began to wonder if William could have been mistaken about Kirsty's supposed relationship. It didn't seem likely that she would have had the chance to meet anyone. She refilled the cups.

'You must get rather depressed at times,' she remarked.

Kirsty shrugged. 'Dad's a very good patient. He's good company too when he isn't feeling too bad. We get along well. Things could be a lot worse.'

'But you haven't felt well lately. Why is that, do you think?'

Kirsty avoided Corrie's eyes. 'Everyone gets tired and tense at times, don't they?'

'Of course.'

'The tranquillisers that Dr Forbes gave me helped,' Kirsty added.

'Good.'

There was a short silence as Kirsty took a handkerchief out of her handbag and carefully unfolded it. Then she said quite suddenly, 'I met him at the supermarket.' She glanced at Corrie. 'I go there once a week, you see—for the shopping,' she added superfluously.

'Him?' queried Corrie.

'His name is Frank. We just sort of kept running into each other. Then one day he asked me to have a coffee with him and it sort of—went from there. He told me he was thirty-two and that he shared a flat with a friend, another fellow. Later I found out that he lived way out in the sticks and was married with two small children, which was why he did the weekly shopping.' The words came out in a rush, leaving her slightly breathless. She paused and looked up at Corrie, a helpless expression in her eyes. 'By then, of course, it was—too late.'

'You'd become fond of him?'

'You could call it that, I suppose.' Kirsty was twisting the handkerchief round her fingers. 'When he told me—about his family—I was shocked and upset. At first I said I wouldn't see him again, but he begged me. He said he was unhappy, that he hadn't known what real love was until he met me. That he hadn't wanted to tell me, but felt he owed me the truth.'

Corrie cringed inwardly. Did they *all* use the same line? 'So you allowed it to drift on?'

'Yes,' the girl sighed. She was beginning to relax now—as though telling her secret was a great weight off her mind. 'We became lovers after a while. At first there was nowhere we could go to be together, then Frank got the key of an empty holiday cottage. He was—*is* an estate agent, you see. We used to go there once a week.' Her lower lip began to quiver. 'I used to look forward to being with him so much. As long as I had our afternoons to look forward to I could put up with anything. On the days we met I'd wake up so *happy* in the mornings. On those days the sun always seemed to shine.' She took a deep breath and steadied her trembling voice. 'Of course I always knew it would have to end some day. There was Dad, for one thing—I couldn't leave him. And then there was Frank's wife—and children. Everything was stacked against us. We never talked about it, though, and I tried not to think of it. Then. . .'

There was a lump in Corrie's throat. The story had such a terrible inevitability about it. She could guess what was coming. 'Yes—then. . .?' she prompted gently.

The girl swallowed hard. 'Then one day he suddenly said it was the last time we'd see each other. He said his wife suspected something. He didn't know how she knew, but somehow she did. He said that as I couldn't leave Dad and he couldn't leave her we'd just hurt everyone by going on, and the awful part was that of course he was right.' She drew a deep, shuddering breath. 'It was as though the world had come to an end for me. Although I knew that what he was saying was right, I begged him not to say it was over—not yet. But he said we must think of her, that she was—was human too.'

'When was this?' Corrie asked.

'Almost a year ago,' Kirsty whispered.

'And you can't forget—still haven't got over it?'

'*No.*' The word was barely audible as Kirsty tried to straighten out her crumpled handkerchief. 'There'd never been anyone else, you see. I'd never—never loved anyone in that way before.' She sighed. 'For a while I really thought I was getting over it. I kept telling myself it was for the best, that it couldn't have lasted, and the thought that he still loved me helped. But then I saw him. It was about six months ago. He was with his wife. She had a tiny new baby in a pram. I knew then that must have been the real reason he said it must end.' She looked up at Corrie. 'It hit me then. I knew suddenly that everything else he'd told me must have been a pack of lies.'

Corrie sighed. 'Kirsty, think—if you could choose, would you *really* have him back again?'

The girl looked up at her in surprise. She opened

her mouth and then closed it again. 'You know, I was just going to say "yes", then I thought—I suddenly realised something.'

'What's that?'

'That the man I loved so much never really existed. It isn't *Frank* I miss, is it? It's just the dream—the fantasy I'd built up around him.'

'Exactly. So what would you wish for now if you could?'

Kirsty considered for a moment. 'I'd like to be free.' She looked up. 'Not free of my responsibilities—of Dad. Free of guilt. I feel so bad, you see; about cheating Frank's wife, about leaving Dad alone to be with him—about—oh, *everything*!'

'And it's the guilt that's making you ill and miserable, not the loss,' Corrie told her. 'But you mustn't feel guilty, Kirsty. You've paid the price. You were the only loser; *you* were the only one who got hurt. I know it isn't easy, but you have to try hard to make a new life now. Isn't there someone who would sit with your father while you went out one night a week?'

The girl looked doubtful. 'Even if there were, where would I go?'

'There must be something you like to do. I hear there's a dance on at the Gordon Arms next week. Why not go to that?'

Kirsty shrank visibly. 'On my own? I wouldn't know anyone. People would think it odd.'

'Why should they? You're an attractive girl, you'd get plenty of partners. And there must be dozens of people you know, even if you've lost touch. If all else fails, I'll be there. You could always come and talk to me.'

'Oh. . .' For a moment Kirsty's eyes lit up, then they clouded again. 'I don't think so.'

Corrie leaned forward. 'You have to break out of that rut, Kirsty,' she said earnestly. 'The first step is the hardest. After that it will start to get easier. Think about it. Don't let Frank have it all his own way. He was the real cheat—he had the best of both worlds. At least you can make the best of the one you have.'

For a long undecided moment Kirsty looked into her eyes, then she said, 'All right, I'll try,' and the expression on her face showed that she meant it. 'If I can find someone to sit with Dad I'll come to that dance. I'll do it.'

Kirsty looked more cheerful as she mounted her bicycle and pedalled away along the track. When she reached the bend that led up on to the road she turned to wave, and Corrie lifted her arm in response. It seemed impossible that they had met for the first time only a little over an hour ago.

Slowly and thoughtfully she walked back round the house and climbed the back stairs to her rooms again. It was a lovely golden late afternoon, with the sun hanging low in a cloudless sky, bathing everything it touched with warm, golden light. Corrie sat at her window, looking out at the view and thinking about Kirsty's touching and tragic story. It was so ridiculously easy to give advice, she told herself angrily; far less easy to take it. For the first time she realised how lucky she was. Like Kirsty, she had been forced to try and make a new life for herself, but it had been so much easier for her. It had been hard to give up the job she had worked for, but at least she'd been free to do it, to remove herself from all the things that reminded her and leave all the painful associations behind her. She had old friends who welcomed her and were willing to help. Kirsty had only her sick father. Like Hugh, the faithless Frank had returned unscathed to his wife and family. No doubt they would both look for new diversions to break the monotony of domesticity once things had died down.

Corrie stood up and straightened her shoulders resolutely. It would be a very long time before she gave her heart again, she promised herself. From now on she would put all her emotional energy into her work. At least there it would not be wasted.

CHAPTER FIVE

IT WAS the rule that the three counsellors did not discuss the people who came to them for advice except under extreme conditions. Corrie was unsure whether the rule included William. Kirsty was his patient, and if he was to treat her successfully he would probably want to know the outcome of the meeting. After Kirsty's visit she had wondered whether to ring him, but finally she decided to wait until he asked. She had thought about the girl a lot since the afternoon they had talked. It seemed such a waste of a young life that she should be shut away from the world as she was. Kirsty was attractive, bright and intelligent. She had so much to offer. But she had a strong sense of duty too, and she clearly loved her father. The answer was almost impossible to find. Corrie was so preoccupied with these thoughts that on the morning after their first meeting Sheila had asked her if anything was wrong.

'You've been miles away all morning. Not homesick, are you?'

They had just come to the end of Sheila's exercise session and were having their coffee. Corrie looked up in surprise.

'Homesick? Good heavens, no. This *is* my home, after all.'

Sheila smiled wryly. 'I think you know what I mean, dear.'

'If you're wondering if I still think about Hugh the answer is yes, I suppose I will for a long time to come. That's something I have to live with. But if I was miles away this morning it was because I was thinking about the young woman I saw yesterday.'

Sheila shook her head. 'You mustn't let them get to you, you know. You can't help unless you can find it in yourself to be objective.'

'Of course, I realise that.' Corrie was silent. She couldn't tell Sheila the reason for her preoccupation was that Kirsty's case was so like her own. 'I'll get used to it,' she smiled. 'Now, have you thought any more about buying that exercise cycle that Christie mentioned?'

'As a matter of fact I have.' Sheila reached out to pull a booklet out of the magazine rack. 'Christie lent me this catalogue and I've been looking through it. Some of these machines look quite fun. Did you know they have digital read-outs to tell you how many "miles" you've done and you can adjust them to go "uphill" to make you work harder?'

Corrie smiled. 'So I believe. You're going to order one, then?'

'Do you know, I believe I will,' Sheila said with a smile. 'Just think how nice it will be in the winter to ride ten miles without getting cold and wet!' She passed Corrie the catalogue. 'See which one you think would suit me best and we'll send off for it this afternoon.' Her eyes twinkled. 'I might even let you have a go on it if you behave yourself.' She drained her coffee-cup and passed it to Corrie to be refilled. 'I understand you're going to the dance at the Gordon Arms with William.'

'Who told you that?' Corrie asked, passing the cup.

'Ah, a little bird.'

'I haven't actually said I'll go yet,' Corrie told her. 'I was going to ask you how you felt about it.'

'How *I* felt? Why should that have any bearing on it?'

'You know I wouldn't go out if you needed me,' Corrie admonished.

Sheila sighed. 'How many times do I have to tell you? Your evenings are your own. You can do as you like—entertain friends in your own room upstairs, go out—whatever. There's no reason why we should be joined at the hip, is there? I like a bit of time to myself too, remember? Now, why don't you ring William now and tell him you'll go?'

'There's no hurry. It won't hurt him to wait.'

Sheila was clearly irritated by Corrie's casual attitude. 'William's a very attractive man, you know. Quite the most eligible man in the neighbourhood.'

'In that case, I'd better leave him alone,' Corrie said with a smile. 'I don't want to add to the competition, do I? Don't particularly want my eyes scratched out.'

Sheila looked thoughtfully at her for a moment. 'You're afraid of being hurt again, aren't you?' she said quietly.

Corrie stood up and picked up the tray. 'I'm not afraid because I don't intend to get involved with anyone again,' she said dismissively. 'If I go out with William or anyone else it will be for company and friendship, nothing else.'

'Well,' said Sheila, half to herself, 'that puts *me* in my place! Stop interfering, Sheila, you old matchmaker!' Nevertheless, there was a glint in her eye, and the moment Corrie was out of the room she picked up the telephone and dialled William's number.

In the kitchen Corrie found Kathy taking her own coffee break after washing the floor.

'Don't get up, Kathy,' she said, putting the used cups into the sink. 'I can wash these.' She glanced curiously at the older woman as she ran hot water into the sink. 'Are you all right? You're not looking your usual cheerful self this morning.'

Kathy sighed. 'It's wee Angus,' she explained.

'Is he ill?'

Kathy sighed. 'That's just it—I don't know. Moira says I fuss about nothing, but it isn't right for a child of his age to be so quiet and well-behaved.'

Corrie laughed. 'Well, that's one complaint I haven't often heard,' she said.

'Exactly—that's just it.' Kathy looked at her. 'Angus started play-school after Easter. Last week Moira was busy, so I picked him up on my way home from here. The teacher asked to have a word with me. She says he doesn't join in but just sits on his own all the time.'

'Perhaps he's shy. He'll settle down,' said Corrie.

'That's what Moira keeps saying, but it confirmed a worry I've had for some time. There's something about the child that just isn't normal. It sounds daft, but he's too *good*. Ian says I'm just being a typical granny, but the bairn doesn't look right to me. Running around seems to wear him out. He gets breathless. He seems so listless and tired, and he's getting worse all the time.'

Corrie hung up the teatowel and sat down opposite

Kathy at the kitchen table. 'That certainly doesn't seem right for a little boy of four. It sounds as though he might be anaemic. Have you asked the doctor about him?'

Kathy shrugged helplessly. 'Ian, my son-in-law, won't hear of it—says if I had my way I'd make an invalid out of the boy.' She sighed. 'Moira and I have always been so close, but it's driving a wedge between us. Every time I mention the child's health it leads to a row. Last night Ian accused me of interfering. But I can't just sit there and say nothing when I'm so worried, can I?'

'Of course you can't.' Corrie smiled reassuringly at her. 'Look, would you like to go off earlier today? I can easily get Mrs Fraser's lunch. Maybe you could have a quiet talk with your daughter while she's on her own, without either of you getting too emotional about it.'

'Oh, could I? That would be a help.' Kathy looked more cheerful. 'If they'd just agree to have the bairn checked over it would ease my mind. Surely Moira can't object to that?'

When she'd gone Corrie thought about Kathy's situation as she began to prepare the lunch. Although she hadn't liked to worry Kathy unnecessarily, she didn't like the sound of the child's symptoms. They could point to any one of several things. The sooner William had a look at him the better, in her view.

Corrie was slightly irritated to discover that Sheila had organised her evening out with William. She had a telephone call from him the following morning.

'Hello there. I got your message. I'm glad you've seen sense.'

She stared at the receiver. 'Sorry, William, but I haven't the faintest idea what you're talking about. What message?'

'The one you asked Sheila to ring me with—to say that you'd like to accept my invitation.'

'But I didn't ask her to give you a message.'

'Come on, now, no need to be shy with me. We've known each other far too long for that,' he said with a chuckle. 'I seem to remember you asked Christie to pass on a message last time we were going to a dance together.'

Corrie bit her lip with annoyance. Was she never to be allowed to forget that childish episode? 'Can I trust you not to take *Sheila* to the dance instead of me, in that case?' she asked cryptically.

'So you *do* remember!' he laughed. 'Can't stop to chat now, Corrie, it's time to start surgery. I'll pick you up at eight on Friday. Make yourself look ravishing for me, eh? Bye!'

He rang off abruptly, and Corrie fumed silently as she hung up the receiver. Sheila had absolutely no right to ring William and say she would go to the dance with him. She toyed with the idea of ringing back to say it was all a mistake, then she remembered her promise to Kirsty that she would be there. She couldn't let the girl down. Make yourself look ravishing for me, he'd said. What a nerve! She'd a good mind to wear the ugliest clothes she could find, put grease on her hair, and go without make-up. *That'd* show him! And she'd give Sheila a piece of her mind, taking matters into her own hands like that.

In the end she hadn't the heart to say too much to Sheila, who seemed ridiculously pleased that she was going to the dance. She supposed she'd meant well and had her best interests at heart. But she did admonish her gently, making it clear that she would not tolerate anyone organising her life for her. Sheila was suitably penitent, promising never to do it again—and waiting until Corrie's back was turned to grin smugly to herself.

Getting ready for the dance, Corrie took out her oldest, most out-of-date dress and hung it on the outside of the wardrobe, looking at it thoughtfully. Why should she dress up to go—under protest—to a village hop with William? Then right at the back she caught sight of the dress she had bought for the hospital dance last January, just about the time that she and Hugh had broken up. It was a lovely dress, made of cream chiffon, and it had cost her the earth. The full skirt was finely pleated and the close-fitting bodice was subtly spangled with silver thread. It was perhaps a little too dressy for this kind of occasion, but with a sudden spark of defiance she pulled it out of the wardrobe and laid it across the bed. She would wear it with plain silver sandals and no jewellery. Why not?

William arrived on the stroke of eight. Corrie heard his voice downstairs and perversely took her time about joining him. Sheila was giving him a glass of whisky in the sitting-room when she came downstairs. As she walked into the room he had his back to her, glass in hand, and she was somewhat taken aback to see that he wore full Highland dress—a splendid kilt in Black Watch tartan, complete with sporran, black velvet jacket with gleaming gilt buttons over an elegant white ruffled shirt. The sight was totally unexpected, and she stood in the doorway for a moment quite stunned with admiration as he stood by the fireplace drinking his whisky. He seemed to fill the small room with his vibrant presence. She was still looking at him when he suddenly turned and noticed her standing there.

'Good evening, William,' she said quietly.

'Oh, hello. . .' His eyes were round with amazement. It was clear as he stared at her that he was as taken aback by her appearance as she was by his.

'Is something wrong?' she asked.

Sheila spoke. 'Corrie, my dear, you look absolutely lovely!' She looked proudly at William. 'And what do you think of William? Isn't he handsome?'

'Very—smart.' Corrie threw the wispy silk shawl she was carrying around her shoulders and looked enquiringly at William. 'Well, are you ready?'

He shook his head slightly, finding his voice at last. 'Oh—er—yes. Thanks for the dram, Sheila.' He crossed the room to take Corrie's arm and turned with a twinkle in his eye. 'Sorry I can't promise to have Cinderella here back by midnight.'

Sheila chuckled. 'Keep her out as late as you like,' she said. 'Have a good time, both of you.'

As they walked to the car he turned to Corrie, his eyes frankly admiring. 'Sheila was right, you *do* look lovely. I can hardly believe you're. . .'

'The little girl who was always tearing her knickers?' she finished for him, guessing he was searching his mind for a put-down. 'Well, if it's any comfort to you, I can hardly believe *you're* the awkward great lump who used to bully me. I see that even your knees are clean nowadays.'

He laughed. 'Walked right into that one, didn't I? Thirty—love, eh?'

She fastened her seatbelt. 'No, love—a. . . I mean a draw, I think.'

William started the car and began to drive along the track, a smile tugging at the corners of his mouth. 'In that case I can't wait for the re-play!'

The large function room at the Gordon Arms had been decked out with bunting and flowers and lit by coloured lights. A sumptuous buffet was laid out in the smaller, adjoining room and a ceilidh band was playing when they arrived. The moment they entered the room William was greeted enthusiastically by at least a dozen or more young women. Before he could introduce Corrie to anyone he was grasped by both hands and drawn into an energetic reel the band had just started to play. Sitting down to watch, Corrie was impressed at William's skill on the floor as he danced the reel with grace and agility. She didn't notice the girl approaching her until she felt a light touch on her arm and looked up to find Kirsty standing next to her.

'Miss Ashley—Corinne!'

'Kirsty! You came, then—I'm so glad. Won't you sit down and join me?'

Kirsty took the chair next to her, following Corrie's gaze as she watched the dancers. 'Dr William dances well, doesn't he?'

'Very,' Corrie agreed. 'I'm just wondering whether I can remember any of the reels I learned at school. I haven't danced them for years. I don't want to look foolish.'

Kirsty laughed. 'You won't. It's like riding a bike or swimming—once you've learned, it comes back naturally.'

'I hope you're right.'

'He looks fine and handsome in the kilt, doesn't he?' Kirsty observed. 'Every female eye in the room is on him.'

Corrie glanced around her and saw that Kirsty was right. She looked again at William. He certainly cut a fine figure on the dance floor. The dark blue and green of the tartan and the black velvet complemented his copper hair, and his shapely, well-muscled legs were shown to advantage as the heavy kilt swung with the movement. Corrie began to wonder how she could live up to his splendid image. She turned to the girl sitting beside her.

'You found a sitter for your father, then?' she asked, changing the subject.

'Yes. My neighbour's husband is playing chess with him. He enjoys that. I won't have to be late home, though.'

'Never mind. You're here, that's the main thing.'

The reel ended and William joined them, smiling. 'Kirsty, how nice to see you here!'

'Good evening, Doctor.' She stood up. 'I'll maybe see you both later. Goodbye now.'

William sat down beside Corrie. 'Did you achieve it?' he asked. 'I don't think that girl has been out to enjoy herself for years. How did you do it?'

'I tried to convince her that she should try to make the sort of life for herself, to make the most of whatever small amount of freedom she can get. She's been out of the swim for so long, poor girl. It must have taken real courage for her to come here this evening.'

He nodded. 'Well, I can't help feeling you must have inspired some of that courage in her. But we'll talk about that later. How about dancing with me now?' He stood up and held out his hand to her as the band began to play again. To her relief, this time it was a waltz they were playing. She stood up and let him lead her on to the floor.

'I'm glad it's not another reel. I think I've forgotten all I ever learned,' she confessed as he drew her close.

'Jimmy Blair and his lads only play until supper,' he told her. 'After that we'll be having some modern music to dance to. On tape, I'm afraid, but the teenagers seem to prefer it.'

Corrie wondered with a silent smile if William was as good at the lambada as he was at the reels, but she decided to wait and see. He drew back his head to look down at her.

'You're smiling—that's a good sign.'

'Go on with you! You make me sound like some kind of Gorgon!' laughed Corrie.

He chuckled. 'No danger of you turning *me* to stone, I promise you! Especially in that dress.' He pulled her a little closer and Corrie felt his laugh vibrate against her.

'You're a good dancer, I'll give you that,' she told him.

'You're pretty nifty on your feet yourself.' His eyes teased her. 'In fact, I'm quite glad I brought you.'

As the evening progressed Christie and Peter

arrived, and with Christie's help Corrie renewed acquaintance with several other old school friends. Everyone had dressed for the occasion, and she was glad she had worn the cream dress. About fifty per cent of the men wore Highland dress, and it was good to see men in kilts again. Corrie remembered some of the farmers wearing the kilt when she was a child, a more sober version of those worn tonight, made of tough thornproof material in muted versions of the dress tartans, and topped by stout tweed jackets.

The music was good and enthusiastically played, and she began to enjoy herself enormously. As Kirsty had said, she found the steps of the reels coming back to her as soon as she began to dance them, and William swung her round in the eightsome so that her feet hardly touched the floor and she was quite dizzy.

Supper came as a welcome respite. There was a delicious spread, crowned by an enormous whole salmon, donated especially, as Corrie learned, by the Laird. It held pride of place in the centre of the table, magnificently decorated and garnished. She and William filled their plates and went to sit at one of the small tables fringing the dance floor.

'What's the dance in aid of?' she asked, sampling her salmon with relish. 'It's obviously some kind of celebration.'

'I'm surprised you don't remember. The town has celebrated the Laird's birthday since time immemorial.'

Corrie frowned. 'As I remember, that celebration took place in November.'

'Ah, but you've been away a long time,' William

reminded her. 'We have a different Laird now. Gavin McLeod inherited his father's estate four years ago.'

'Ah, of course. I'm out of touch, aren't I?' Corrie smiled wryly.

'We'll have you up to date with everything in no time—if you stay long enough.' He looked at her enquiringly, his eyes suddenly serious. 'You *will* be staying, won't you, Corrie?'

She grinned and adopted a heavy Highland accent as she replied, 'Aye, Dr Forbes, I'll be staying right enough. I'm liking it here just fine.'

He laughed and reached across the table to squeeze her fingers. 'Great! Now, can I get you a wee dram to wash down your supper, Miss Ashley?'

She shook her head. 'Maybe one of us should lay off the drams. It would never do for the local doctor to get breathalysed, now would it?'

William looked at her askance. 'No one gets breathalysed in Glencarron on the Laird's birthday, woman. It would be tantamount to sacrilege!'

'Well, just a wee one, then. But you'd better make if *very* wee. I think I shall feel safer if *I* drive home.'

When William had gone to get the drinks Corrie saw Kirsty talking to a young man. The girl seemed to be enjoying herself. Her cheeks were pink and she looked extremely pretty. Seeing Corrie looking in her direction, she came across.

'I'm away home now, Miss Ashley,' she said. 'Thank you for persuading me to come. I've had a great time.'

'I hope it'll be the first of many.' Corrie glanced over the girl's shoulder to where the young man stood waiting. 'Have you a lift home?' she asked.

Kirsty nodded. 'Brian's taking me. We were at school together. I told him not to spoil the evening, leaving early, but he insists he doesn't mind.'

'Well, I'm glad. Goodnight, Kirsty. And remember, any time you want to talk—about anything at all, you know where I am.'

Kirsty smiled. 'Thanks. I'll remember.'

William returned just in time to see her leaving, and as he sat down he asked Corrie, 'She enjoyed herself, then?'

'Yes, but she has to get back to her father now.'

'Did she say much to you last week—unburden herself?'

Corrie nodded. 'Do you want me to tell you?'

'No, perhaps better not,' he said.

'You were right about her, though,' Corrie told him. 'I think you should know that much. She's had a very bad time—been desperately unhappy. But I think she'll be all right now.'

'That's fine. Thanks, Corrie. As a matter of fact, there's another case I'd like. . .' He broke off as a sudden commotion on the other side of the room attracted everyone's attention. 'Ah, it's the Laird. He usually puts in an appearance around now. We'll all be required to drink his health, then he usually has one dance and then leaves.'

Gavin McLeod was another vaguely remembered acquaintance of Corrie's childhood, although he had been away at boarding school for much of the time. But she hardly recognised the tall, handsome man who had just entered the room. He wore his glossy dark hair a little longer than most of the other men in the room and he was wearing a dinner jacket and black tie. Corrie guessed he had just come from a family dinner. Waitresses brought round trays with glasses of champagne for everyone, and they all drank the Laird's health, then Jimmy Blair's band played for the traditional celebratory sword dance, performed by one of their number to rousing cheers. When it was over and the excitement had died down they played a waltz, and to Corrie's surprise Gavin walked straight across the room to where she sat and asked her to dance. As they circled the floor he smiled down at her.

'As far as I know I haven't seen you before, so what makes me feel that you're no stranger?'

She laughed. 'Probably because I'm not. I grew up in Glencarron. I'm Corinne Ashley. My father was Dr Ashley.'

'Of course, Corrie—I remember now. I used to ogle you in church on Sundays.'

'Did you?'

He drew down the corners of his mouth. 'You mean I was wasting my time—you never noticed? I'm devastated!'

While they were dancing Corrie was acutely aware of William's eyes on them. When the dance was over and Gavin was escorting her back to their table he said, 'I hope I haven't offended Dr Forbes, borrowing his partner without asking?'

'Not at all,' Corrie told him with a smile. 'I make my own decisions, and after all, it is your birthday.'

'A woman after my own heart,' he said gallantly, raising her hand to his lips. 'Thank you for an enchanting dance. I hope we meet again soon, Corrie.'

As Gavin walked away William glared after him.

'Old smoothie! He might have asked permission,' he growled.

Corrie stared at him. '*Permission*? He did. I said yes.' She raised an eyebrow at him. 'Or could you have meant *your* permission?'

William cleared his throat loudly and took her arm. 'Shall we go now, before the disco thing begins?'

Her eyes sparkled wickedly as she looked at him. 'William Forbes. I do believe you're chickening out! Is modern dancing too much for those rustic Scottish legs of yours?'

'Right, Corinne Ashley.' As the first tune began to blare out and the floor filled with teenagers William took her arm determinedly. 'Fasten your safety-belt. And remember, you asked for this!'

William proved that he was as adept at modern dancing as he was at reels, and by the time the tune ended Corrie was breathless.

'OK, I give in,' she gasped as they came back to their seats. 'Where did you learn to dance like that?'

'You're not the only one who trained in a big city hospital,' he reminded her. 'I used to be known as Edinburgh's answer to John Travolta, I'll have you know.'

She shook her head, still laughing breathlessly. 'Right, you've proved your point. Maybe we'd better go now.'

Outside the air was cool after the heat inside. Corrie shivered slightly and wrapped the flimsy silk shawl around her shoulders. William looked at her and shook his head.

'Why do women always wear such damned silly clothes?' he asked. 'There isn't enough warmth in that thing to keep a sparrow from pneumonia!' He reached into the back of the car and drew out a large hairy rug, wrapping it round her. As he pulled it around her shoulders his fingers brushed her cheek. She looked up at him and their eyes held for a moment. William said softly, 'Thank you for coming with me this evening, Corrie.'

'Thank you for bringing me. I've had a lovely time.'

'I asked you to make yourself look ravishing. I bet you thought it was a cheek, but you did me proud just the same.'

She shook her head, smiling wryly as she remembered her first intentions and grateful that she hadn't adhered to them. 'Wearing this dress was an impulse,' she confessed. 'It was bought for a special occasion. I've only worn it once before. It didn't have very happy memories.'

Holding the edges of the shawl, he pulled her closer. 'It'd be nice to think that maybe the memories are happier now.'

She smiled. 'Yes, they are.'

He paused a moment, then tipped her chin up and kissed her gently. This time she didn't shrink from him, but responded warmly. He gave a little groan of satisfaction and wrapped his arms around her, resting his cheek against her hair. 'Would it surprise you to know that I've been dying to do that all evening?' When she didn't reply he kissed her again.

'You're warmer now,' he whispered against her cheek. 'Much warmer.'

She stirred in his arms. 'William, I think perhaps we should go now.'

They drove for a while in silence, then he pulled

the car over and stopped. Switching off the engine, he turned to her. 'Can we talk? Just for a while?'

'About what?'

Her eyes were huge and luminous in the moonlight and he laughed softly. 'It's all right, I know how you feel, and I'm not rushing you into anything. My intentions are strictly honourable—for now, anyway.'

She smiled. 'I'm delighted to hear it.'

He looked at her for a long moment. 'I thought you might want to talk.'

'What makes you think that?'

'It does us all good to talk. You proved that with Kirsty, didn't you?'

'Are you offering to counsel me, Dr Forbes?'

He slipped an arm along the back of the seat. 'I wouldn't presume to offer any such thing. But I'd like us to be friends, Corrie—close friends. Is that what you'd like too?'

'Yes, William.'

His hand cupped her shoulder and pulled her close, drawing her head down on to his shoulder. 'Right. That's what friends are for, isn't it—confiding in?' When she didn't reply he said, 'Of course, if you don't feel you can trust me. If you'd rather not. . .'

'William, there isn't much to tell. I fell in love with an older man—a surgeon I worked with. Hugh was someone else's husband. It was wrong, and as I should have known it would, it blew up in my face. I'm still paying the price. It cost me my job, my self-respect, my confidence. . .' She sighed. 'That's all there is to it.'

'Except that it *isn't*.' He pressed his lips briefly against her temple. 'You've been unhappy, which is why you understood what Kirsty had been through. That proves that it wasn't quite for nothing.' He turned her face so that he could look into her eyes. 'Was *he* hurt? Was anyone else's life upset?'

She shook her head. 'No. Neither in my case or Kirsty's was a marriage broken.'

'Just your heart?'

'Just my heart. But I'm learning to live with the pieces,' she told him firmly. 'The rough edges are beginning to wear smooth.'

'I know how it feels,' he said softly. 'Corrie, let me help you pick up the pieces?'

After a pause she said, 'And suppose they won't fit together again?'

'Oh, they will,' he told her. 'Sometimes they fit together in a slightly different way, but they'll fit together again all right. I'm an expert on hearts.'

She smiled up at him. 'In that case, I'd appreciate your help very much.'

'Great!'

To her relief he didn't attempt to kiss her again but started the car and drove on. In the soft light Corrie smiled. Tonight she had enjoyed herself more than she remembered doing for a long time. Both she and William had been hurt, but she was sure they were both far too sensible to rush into anything on the rebound. Friends, he had said. Close friends. And close friends they would be. For the first time in months she suddenly realised that she was actually happy.

CHAPTER SIX

'AND I'M told that the Laird singled you out to dance with.' Sheila was all agog over breakfast next morning, wanting to hear every tiny detail of the dance at the Gordon Arms.

Corrie looked up from her breakfast, her eyes wide with surprise. 'That's right. But how on earth did you know?'

Sheila laughed. 'I was down early this morning and I happened to be out in the front when Andrew Magee came. He's the postie and he told me. He was at the dance too. Apparently it's the talk of the place this morning.'

Corrie shook her head. 'News certainly travels fast around here! I'm surprised there's any need for a postal service. Yes, Gavin McLeod did ask me to dance. I remembered him from the old days, though I hadn't realised that he was Laird now.'

Sheila smiled as she spread a piece of crispbread. 'And what did William think of that?'

'I shouldn't think he gave it a thought, one way or the other,' said Corrie, refusing to rise to the bait.

'Gavin's a very handsome, sophisticated man. There isn't a girl in Glencarron who wouldn't give her eye teeth for the chance to go out with him,' Sheila said.

Corrie laughed. 'Oh? I thought William had the honour of being the most eligible bachelor in town.'

Sheila shrugged. 'Oh, well, William is much more *available* than the Laird. I dare say there's some aristocratic beauty in line for the honour of becoming *his* wife in the fullness of time.' She pulled a face. 'Personally I don't trust that type myself. He'll have his work cut out living up to his father's reputation. A lovely man, Duncan McLeod; he was like a father to the people of Glencarron.'

'Gavin seemed very nice and really quite ordinary, I thought,' Corrie said. 'If a little on the smooth side.' She glanced at the clock. 'Sheila, we'd better get your exercise session over with. Had you forgotten that it's this morning that Christie is bringing her reflexologist friend to see you?'

Sheila frowned with annoyance. 'Damn, I had forgotten. And I was planning to paint this morning too.'

'How's your vision?' Corrie asked. 'Do you think it might interfere with your drawing and painting?'

'I don't really know till I try, do I?' Sheila said resignedly. 'I do hope all this isn't going to prove a waste of time. What miracle this person can hope to perform just by tickling my feet, heaven alone knows.' She heaved herself out of her chair with a sigh. 'The indignities one has to go through for the sake of. . .'

'Sheila!' Corrie gave her a warning glance.

'I know—count my blessings,' Sheila smiled. 'And I admit that I do have more than most. Don't think I don't appreciate all of you and what you do for me, because I do.'

Christie's car drew up at eleven o'clock. Sheila was watching for her from the sitting-room window and Corrie heard her exclaim. She looked up.

'What is it?' she asked.

'It's Christie's friend. She's Indian and quite beautiful. Come and see.'

Corrie went across to glance out of the window and saw Christie coming up the steps, accompanied by a tall, slim young woman in a graceful pink sari. She wore her hair in a thick glossy black braid which fell to her waist and she had the most beautiful, serene face Corrie had ever seen. She turned to smile at Sheila.

'I have a feeling you're going to enjoy this morning,' she said. 'I'll go and tell Kathy to put the coffee on.'

Mrs Rhani Patel surprised them by having a pronounced Scottish accent. Over coffee she told them she had grown up in Glasgow where her parents had a newsagent's shop. The family had come to Britain from Uganda when Rhani was very small, but she had moved to the Highlands with her husband several years ago when he had come to work in a hospital in Inverness.

'Rhani's husband is a physiotherapist,' Christie explained. 'He and I often work together.'

'Perhaps I'd better explain a little about reflexology,' Rhani told them. 'It's becoming quite a recognised therapy now. Some hospitals are even training their physiotherapists to do it. We work on the feet, as you know, and it's very much along the same lines as acupuncture—except that we don't stick needles into our patients!' She smiled reassuringly at Sheila. 'By applying gentle pressure to certain points of the feet energies are released throughout the nervous system to culminate in the brain. It's part of holistic medicine—treating the whole person, rather than one or two symptoms. We can eliminate pain and stress, relax the body, and we're often able to diagnose problems that have been overlooked. Each part of the body has its own area on the foot.' She smiled. 'So, if you're ready, shall we begin?'

Corrie watched with fascination as the strong but gentle hands handled Sheila's feet. There was confidence and expertise in Rhani's touch and when she reached Sheila's second toe she looked up enquiringly.

'You're experiencing visual problems?'

Sheila gasped. 'Why, yes. Did Christie tell you?'

Rhani smiled and shook her head. 'I especially asked Christie to tell me nothing. It's better for me to let the feet tell everything.' She wiggled Sheila's second toe. 'Here's the little telltale. I shall work on him, and along the sides here.' She ran her fingers down the inner side of Sheila's foot. 'This area represents the spine, where I can feel there are many problems.'

By the time the treatment was finished Sheila was relaxed, hardly able to keep awake, in fact, and Rhani suggested that a little rest before lunch would be beneficial. When she had gone upstairs she looked at Corrie.

'You're her nurse?' she asked.

'Yes.'

'Then I can tell you my findings. Her central nervous system is affected. I would say she's in the early stages of MS.'

'You're right. I'm impressed,' Corrie said. 'And I'm sure you've done Sheila a lot of good. Will you come again?'

'If she asks me. She would benefit from two treatments a week.' Rhani stood up. 'Of course, I can't offer a cure any more than the doctors can, but I do feel confident that I can help her to live a little more pleasantly.'

While Sheila rested Corrie went into the kitchen to help Kathy with the lunch preparations. While they worked she told the other woman about the reflexologist. Kathy was as impressed as she had been, but she still looked a little preoccupied.

'How's little Angus?' Corrie asked her. 'Did you persuade your daughter to take him to the doctor?'

Kathy nodded. 'She made an appointment for this morning. I can't wait to hear what he said. I'll be calling in to see them on my way home.'

'At least your mind will be set at rest,' said Corrie. 'And if there's any little problem I'm sure it will soon be put right.'

But she didn't feel as confident as she sounded, and when William looked in just after Kathy had left she asked him about the little boy.

He looked concerned. 'I did see him this morning,' he told her. 'His mother brought him along to the surgery rather reluctantly. She said her mother had been nagging her.'

'So you think Kathy's fears are more than just a natural anxiety?'

'I certainly do. In spite of the fact that the child has had every care and attention since birth his development is way below standard. He's underweight too for his age. Then there's the breathlessness.'

'Asthma?' Corrie asked, but William shook his head.

'Strictly between ourselves, Corrie, I suspect a cardiac problem.'

'Oh, no! Poor little boy!'

'I've telephoned for an appointment with the cardiologist in Inverness,' he went on. 'I'd like to have him thoroughly checked out as soon as possible.'

'Kathy's daughter must have been devastated,' remarked Corrie.

'Naturally I played it down as much as I could,' William said. 'Obviously I didn't want to frighten her. After all, I could be wrong. But the child isn't anaemic, his kidneys seem fine and there's no sign of asthma. All I could detect was a murmur. I'm hoping it may be just a blocked valve. That's a relatively simple operation and very successful nowadays, as of course you know.'

'Was there no sign of it at birth?'

He shook his head. 'This kind of thing often doesn't manifest itself till the child begins to get active.' He smiled. 'Anyway, let's look on the bright side and hope for the best. It's good that Kathy noticed.'

'She's been dreadfully worried. She said her daugher and son-in-law wouldn't have it that anything was wrong with little Angus.'

William shook his head. 'Moira *is* worried—that much is very clear. Angus means so much to her and Ian. She can't have any more children, you see, and I rather think they've both been burying their heads in the sand. She seemed very tense and nervy when she came to see me this morning.' He looked thoughtful. 'Maybe it'd be a good idea if you had a word with her.'

'Me? But why?' queried Corrie.

'You've worked with some of the best cardiac surgeons in the country. You could reassure her.'

'Well, of course I'll do whatever I can if you really think I can help.'

Sheila appeared at that moment. She looked bright-eyed and refreshed for her sleep. She looked at William with a twinkle in her eyes.

'So you're here to see how my reflexology session went, are you? Or have you come to check that Corrie hasn't run off with Gavin McLeod?'

She insisted that William should join them for lunch and regaled him with her account of the reflexology treatment, insisting that she hadn't felt so well for months, and that there was a distinct improvement in her vision. William smiled and said, with a sly wink at Corrie, 'Of course, it couldn't have anything to do with the diet Corrie devised for you, or Christie's exercise programme, could it? Not to mention *my* tender loving care.'

Sheila reached across the table to slap him on the wrist. 'William Forbes, you know quite well that I couldn't exist without the three of you. That goes without saying.'

'And I should jolly well think so too,' he said with mock indignation.

Sheila looked from one to the other of them, then asked, 'And when will you two be going out together again?'

Corrie shot her a look, which Sheila carefully avoided. William said, 'As a matter of fact, there's someone I'd rather like you to meet, Corrie. I was going to ask if you'd be free this evening.'

'Of course she is,' Sheila put in.

'Who is it?' Corrie asked guardedly.

'Morag Kincaid.'

'Old Morag? I remember her,' said Corrie. 'We used to be terrified of her as children. She's a recluse, isn't she?'

'She is indeed, and if you're going to that croft of hers you'd better take some clothes pegs,' Sheila advised.

Corrie looked mystified. 'Clothes pegs?'

'For your noses,' Sheila explained. 'Old Morag's more than a bit eccentric. Years ago I dare say she'd have been accused of being a witch. She prefers wild animals to people, and the croft is usually full of sick or injured ones she's treating with her herbs and potions—hence the smell.'

'Oh, she's a harmless enough old body,' said William. 'And say what you will, she has a wonderful way with wild creatures. I used to spend quite a lot of time helping with her animals when I was a kid. We've been friends ever since.'

'Is there a problem with her, William?' Corrie asked.

'Just that she isn't getting any younger. No one knows how old she really is—I'm not sure she even knows herself. Last winter she had a bad bout of bronchitis and her chest has been weak ever since. I'd like to get something done about that old croft before next winter. It's cold and draughty and appallingly damp. But it's on McLeod land.'

'Have you approached the Laird?' Corrie asked.

William sighed. 'I have—just this morning. He wasn't very sympathetic. He pointed out that she should really be in a home at her age, and basically I agree with him. But she'd die, away from her beloved animals.'

'Of course she would,' Sheila put in. 'Duncan McLeod would never have suggested such a thing. I heard that Gavin had applied for planning permission to make those tumbledown old crofts on his land into smart holiday cottages,' she added suspiciously. 'Morag's is the only one occupied. Maybe he wants her out so that he can carry out his plans.'

William chuckled. 'I can't see many holidaymakers staying for long in the vicinity of Morag's croft,' he said. 'At least, not downwind of it!'

'Exactly,' Sheila said triumphantly. 'That's why he'd like to see her carted safely off into a home. But if I know Morag he'll not get his way without a fight.' She looked at Corrie, her blue eyes glinting with the light of battle. 'Go and see her with William this evening,' she said. 'See what you can do to help.'

Morag's croft was reached by a long trek across a stretch of bracken-covered moorland. Forewarned by William, Corrie dressed sensibly in jeans, an Aran sweater and sturdy boots. They drove as far as they could, then climbed a gate and set off across the moorland. Corrie's first sight of the croft brought a gasp of dismay to her lips. The thatched roof was disintegrating and hung down in wisps over the tiny windows. It had been mended with sheets of rusty corrugated iron that were rotting fast. It was difficult to believe that anyone could actually live in such a place.

'What does she do for water?' she asked.

'The burn.' William pointed to where it crossed the moor on its way to the loch.

'And sanitation?'

He grinned. 'The time-honoured method.'

She frowned. 'The Laird should really re-house her.'

'In all fairness, why should he? As far as I know she's never paid a penny in rent.'

'Mmm, I see.' Corrie stared at the almost derelict building. 'But he does have a point about her being better off in a home, doesn't he?'

'Of course he does. I told you—basically, I agree with him. But Morag has lived like this all her life. She must be over eighty. She'll never change now. You'll see what I mean in a minute.'

As they neared the croft a powerful animal smell wafted out through the open door and mingled with the scent of woodsmoke coming from the tumbledown chimney.

'She's got a fox in there with a broken leg,' William told her. 'And a marten she found caught in a trap. There are usually a few birds too, suffering from this or that—all kept in makeshift pens and cages.' He stooped to look in at the door, narrowing his eyes to peer through the smoky gloom inside. 'Morag, I've brought someone to see you—a friend.'

From inside Corrie heard a croaky voice call, 'Who is it?'

'It's me—Dr William.'

From the darkness inside the croft an old woman emerged. She was small and bent and her face was as brown and wrinkled as a walnut, but the eyes that peered at them were as bright and black as a

robin's. She wore a strange assortment of clothes—
stout boots on her feet, a pair of trousers that looked
as though they had been made for a fisherman, and
a thick brown sweater. Wisps of white hair were
escaping from the knitted hat pulled down low over
her ears. She smiled, showing jagged brown stumps
of teeth.

'Well, well, so it's you, Wullie Forbes.' Her
Highland accent was as thick as Scotch broth. 'Come
away in, but dinna shout s'much. Ma beasties are noo
fond o' company, ye ken.' She narrowed her eyes and
peered at Corrie. 'Who's the lassie?'

'This is Corrie Ashley. Remember her father, Dr
Ashley?'

Morag cackled. 'Aye, I mind him well. So this is
his lassie?' She came up close to Corrie and looked at
her intently, studying every feature with darting eyes.
Suddenly she snatched at her arm. 'Gimme your
hand, child.'

Startled, Corrie took a step backwards, but the old
woman had grasped her hand and held it in a vicelike
grip. She opened it and bent her head low over it till
her nose was almost touching the palm. Corrie hardly
dared breathe during the long pause that followed,
and when the old head jerked upwards she started
again.

'Och, ye've been gey heartsore, lassie,' Morag said
softly, looking deep into Corrie's eyes. 'There's been a
lot o' tears for ye. But a' that's done wi'. There's a
braw laddie waitin' who'll mak' ye a fine man and gi'
ye' some bonny bairns.'

Corrie felt William's eyes on her and dared not
meet them. She sensed that he was silently shaking

with laughter and she felt the colour rise in her cheeks. Old Morag looked up at her.

'Ah, I'm right, then? Ye *have* been treated sore?'

'How did you know?' Corrie whispered.

Morag cackled. 'A gift, lassie—like the healin'.' She looked at William. 'Ye'll tak a bite o' supper wi' me? The broth's freshly made.'

A huge black cooking pot like a witch's cauldron bubbled on the open peat fire, and Corrie felt her stomach churn. She shot an appealing look at William, but to her surprise he nodded eagerly.

'I will indeed, Morag. Nothing like your broth to set a man up.' He gave Corrie an encouraging nod as the old woman hobbled over to the dresser to take down bowls. 'It's all right,' he whispered. 'She's spotlessly clean, in spite of the way the place looks. And the broth really is good.'

Corrie found he was right. The broth was delicious and tasty, thick with barley, herbs and fresh vegetables. Morag told them it contained no meat.

'I couldna bring mysel' tae eat ma wee brothers and sisters,' she explained simply.

When they had finished she invited them to look at her 'patients'. The fox, which had a damaged ear as well as a broken leg, was so tame it took scraps of food from her hand.

'He's near enough cured now. In a day or so I'll tak' him up on Craecuillin an' gi' 'im back his freedom,' Morag told them. The marten had lost part of its foot in the trap from which she had freed it.

'It was festerin' sore when I brought him home and the poor mite was near tae starvin', but I got 'im right,' she told them proudly. 'He'll no' go far, but he'll fend for himsel'. He'll know old Morag'll no' see him hungry.'

As well as the animals there was a baby owl with a broken wing and a gull with one leg, both of which seemed to be thriving on Morag's treatment.

'Do you manage to tame all the wild animals you treat?' Corrie asked.

'Most. The only beast I didnae manage so well was a wildcat,' Morag said with a grin. 'She tried to escape and got stuck halfway up the lum. A fine dance she led me! That was the one time I nearly had meat in ma stew. She fell in the pot, ye ken.' The old woman cackled heartily until the laughing ended in a bout of wheezy coughing. William frowned.

'That cough is no better, Morag. Did you take the capsules I gave you?'

She shook her head. 'Och, ye know I dinna hold wi' your drugs, Wullie. I know ye mean well enough, but I'll heal mysel' my own road or not at a'. When ma time comes an' Mither Earth has done wi' me, there's nothin'll keep me here.'

'And what do you think all your animal friends would do without you?' William asked.

She sighed. 'Ah, that's ma only regret, Wullie—ma only regret.'

Walking back across the moor, Corrie asked, 'What will become of her?'

William shook his head. 'She'll die naturally one of these days—just as her animal friends do. You can see what I mean about putting her into a home?'

'Of course. It would be sheer cruelty.'

'All the same, I wish she'd take the penicillin I prescribed for her,' he said. 'She has faith in her herbal treatments, but I have an idea there isn't one that will work on that cough.'

'Maybe she knows that,' said Corrie. 'Maybe she'd rather let nature take its course, as she said. She's an amazing old woman.'

They walked for a few minutes in silence, then William said, 'You haven't been to visit Dad and me since you've been here. What about you and Sheila coming for dinner one evening?'

She turned to smile at him. 'That would be nice. I'm sure Sheila would like it too.'

'Good. I'll talk to Dad about it and we'll arrange something.'

They'd reached the gate and climbed over. William held out his hand to help her down, and as he looked up at her his eyes twinkled.

'I'd give a lot to know who this braw laddie is who's going to give you all those bonny bairns.'

She pushed away the hand he offered. 'I was waiting for that, William Forbes. You never miss a trick, do you?'

He laughed. 'Sorry, I couldn't resist it. You were really quite honoured, though. Morag doesn't tell everyone's fortune, even if they ask her. Here, don't be so stuffy, woman. Let me help you.' Putting his hands firmly round her waist, he swung her down from the gate. As her feet touched the ground she stumbled a little, her hands on his shoulders, and he pulled her close. She looked up at him.

'William. . .' Before she could continue his mouth was on hers. His kiss was warm and searching. She relaxed against the hard strength of his body and surrendered to its demand, responding—comforted—

finally aroused. With a sudden stab of alarm she pushed him gently away.

'We—we'd better be getting back. Sheila will be. . .'

'Sheila would be delighted if she could see us now,' William told her, pulling her firmly back into his arms. 'Don't you know she's been trying to get us together ever since you arrived?'

Corrie laughed shakily. 'I'd have to have been blind not to have seen that!'

'Well then. . .?'

'I know, but. . .' He was kissing her again, pulling her close against him, parting her lips gently with his tongue to kiss her more intimately. Corrie wrenched herself free.

'No, William—no!'

He took her head between his hands, his fingers weaving firmly into the thick curls to hold her captive. 'What is it, Corrie?' The green eyes were dark as they searched hers. 'You don't object to my kissing you, in fact you like it. We've known each other a long time, Corrie. Do you think I can't read your responses? You're a warm, lovely girl. What could be more natural? What are you so afraid of?'

'I'm not——It's just—just that I don't want to get involved again—so soon after. . .'

'Would it help if I were to say "I love you"?' He was still holding her head and she put up her arms to free herself, her cheeks flushing an angry pink.

'What do you think I am, William? Some silly star-struck schoolgirl? I don't need words—flattery—a *sop*. You think you know me, but if you understood me at all you'd have known that. You said the other night that we'd be friends—close friends. Well, that's fine. Why can't we just leave it at that?'

Holding her by the shoulders, he shook her gently. 'It can never stop at that between a normal man and woman. You know that as well as I do. Anyway. . .' his eyes teased her gently '. . .is there any reason why friends can't be lovers too?'

Suddenly something about the look in his eyes seemed to dash all the breath from her. All the protest went out of her and she leaned against him weakly. 'Oh, William, can't you see that what I'm trying to say is that I don't want us to turn to each other in some kind of—of *rebound* reaction?'

His arms closed round her. 'All right. We'll take it a step at a time.' He pressed his lips against her forehead. 'But I warn you,' he whispered, 'I'm not a patient man—especially not where you're concerned.'

Later that night, as she lay in bed with the sound of the burn under her window, Corrie thought about William and what he had said. If she were truthful with herself she had enjoyed his kisses. It was true that she found William attractive and fun to be with, and of course it was good to feel wanted and admired again. But that was just a natural feminine feeling and had nothing to do with deeper emotions. Surely it had more to do with the mending of her damaged confidence—her broken heart? William too had suffered rejection. He had admitted to her that he knew the feeling. And hadn't she heard about his unhappy love affair from his father and from Christie? He too was probably vulnerable. It wouldn't do for either of them to imagine they were falling in love. That could only lead to more unhappiness for both of them. Perhaps she should try to avoid seeing so much of him in future.

But the burn soon began to work its lullaby magic, blurring the troubled pictures in her mind and soothing her to sleep. And as it did so it was William's eyes that haunted the fringes of her consciousness. Those eyes that could laugh and tease, yet gave occasional glimpses of a more serious, much more complex William in their sea-green depths. In the moment before sleep overtook her, Hugh's face usually swam mockingly behind her closed eyelids. Tonight she felt instead the strength of William's arms, the hardness of his body as he held her close, the masculine roughness of his cheek against hers. And last of all, as the velvet darkness closed in, the exciting sweetness of his mouth on hers.

CHAPTER SEVEN

ON THE day that the exercise cycle arrived Christie was at Glencoe House carrying out Sheila's monthly check and updating her exercise programme. When it was done and Christie had pronounced her much improved, Sheila went off to get changed, inviting Christie to stay on for coffee and help her unpack and examine the new toy.

As the door closed behind her Christie turned to Corrie with a smile. 'She's doing fine,' she said. 'The exercises have firmed up her weak muscles and they're gradually getting her out of the bad posture habits she had—helping her to sit, stand and balance better. And she says she's been sleeping more restfully since I showed her better ways to position herself for sleeping.'

'She's quite taken with the idea of this cycle,' Corrie remarked, beginning to unwrap the large parcel.

'Yes. When she comes down we'll look at that,' said Christie. 'I hear she's arranged to have a weekly session with Rhani too.' She smiled. 'I think between us we've got Sheila's MS stabilised and under almost perfect management.'

Corrie looked thoughtful. 'I wouldn't be surprised if she decides soon that she doesn't need me any more.' It was the first time the thought had occurred to her, and she wondered briefly just how she would feel at the prospect of leaving Glencarron. But before she had time to explore the possibility too far Sheila came back into the room and enthusiastically set about unpacking the newly arrived bicycle and trying it out.

It was about an hour later in the kitchen that Corrie found Kathy in tears. She had seemed perfectly composed when she brought in coffee for the three of them earlier, even joining in the excitement as Sheila tried out her newest acquisition. But now, to Corrie's dismay, she found her with tears trickling down her cheeks as she prepared vegetables for lunch.

'*Kathy*, what is it?' she demanded.

'It's wee Angus. Dr William thinks he might have something wrong with his heart. He's to see a specialist in Inverness tomorrow.'

Corrie slipped an arm round the shaking shoulders. 'Don't upset yourself, Kathy. If something is wrong then it's better that it's diagnosed now, and put right as soon as possible.'

'I know that', said Kathy. 'It's Moira—she seems to blame *me*. It's almost as though she thinks I've wished it on the child.' She gave a strangled sob. 'I love that bairn more than my own life, Miss Ashley. I'd give everything I have to make him well. How can she think it of me?'

Corrie helped the older woman to a chair and made her sit down. 'Kathy, Moira's frightened,' she said gently. 'She doesn't mean what she says. I expect she knows quite well that taking Angus to the hospital for tests is for the best. She just needs someone to hit out at because of her fears. And mothers always seem to have to bear the brunt of these things.' Seeing Kathy fumbling in her overall pocket for a handkerchief, she took out a clean tissue and handed it to her. 'Dry your eyes. Now, listen; I used to be a theatre sister in a cardiac unit and I worked with a lot of heart surgeons. I've seen them do some wonderful things. Would you like me to have a talk with Moira?'

Kathy looked up with hope in the brimming eyes, 'Oh, *would* you, Miss Ashley? I'd be so grateful.'

'Of course I will—if you think she'll come. Maybe she'll think I'm interfering too.'

'Oh, I don't think so,' said Kathy. 'Not when I tell her you've worked with these doctors. When can she come?'

'It'd better be soon as the appointment is tomorrow. This afternoon, if she can make it.'

'I'll tell her. I can sit with the wee laddie while she comes.' Kathy took Corrie's hand and squeezed it. 'Thank you, Miss Ashley. You don't know what it means to me.'

Sheila was only too glad for Corrie to see Moira when she told her about the problem. She even went a step further and made a helpful suggestion.

'Maybe the girl would like you to go to the hospital with her,' she said. 'You could take the Rover and drive her there. You know what the local public transport is like. It would save the girl a lot of time and trouble when she's so worried.' She smiled. 'Why not take Kathy too? She can have a day off tomorrow. Walter has just rung and invited us both to dinner tomorrow evening, so I shan't need to eat much at lunchtime.'

'That's very generous of you,' Corrie remarked.

Sheila smiled. 'That's one thing about illness—it makes you feel more for other people.'

* * *

Moira arrived that afternoon at three. Corrie had met her once before, at the Laird's birthday dance, so the two were not strangers. Moira was a small, plump woman, very like her mother. But the round, normally serene face was etched with lines of strain today and her brown eyes were red-rimmed from sleeplessness.

Corrie took her up to her own sitting-room and put the kettle on for the inevitable cup of tea.

'You're taking Angus to see the cardiac consultant tomorrow, then?' she said.

'Aye. And I tell you, Miss Ashley, I'm dreading it.'

'Call me Corrie, please,' Corrie smiled as she handed the girl a cup of tea. 'Is your husband going with you?'

'No. He can't get time off from his work. Things have been difficult lately—a lot of men are being laid off at the fishing. We don't need any more problems.'

'Of course not. In that case, would you like me to take you? Mrs Fraser has offered to let us have the car.'

The girl's eyes lit up. 'Oh, that would be great. . .' She bit her lip. 'Oh, but Ian mightn't like it. He's very independent.'

'In that case we'll let him pay for the petrol,' said Corrie. 'He surely can't object to your being saved all that waiting around for buses and trains?'

'Well, no, I suppose not. It's very kind of you both.'

'Not at all.' Corrie refilled Moira's cup. 'Did your mother tell you I used to work with heart surgeons in the operating theatre of a cardiac unit?'

'Yes.' Moira looked at Corrie anxiously. 'Did you ever see a child as young as Angus with a heart complaint?'

'Many, many times,' Corrie told her. 'And some even younger. I've see them come into hospital weak and pale, with no energy—sometimes with breathing problems. And I've seen them go home later rosy-cheeked and running around like any other child.'

Moira's eyes brimmed. 'Angus is everything in the world to all of us. If anything happened to him. . .'

Corrie touched her hand. 'It won't. Put your trust in the surgeon. Believe me, Moira, diagnosing Angus's problem now, while he's still young, is the best thing that could happen. By the time he's ready for school he'll have had time to make a complete recovery.'

'You—don't think he'll be an—an invalid for the rest of his life?'

Corrie shook her head. 'No, I don't.'

'And the operation—isn't it dangerous?'

'Moira,' Corrie took the girl's hand and held it firmly, 'all operations carry a risk. That's a fact we have to face. But technology has made such leaps and bounds over the past few years that the risk is getting smaller and smaller all the time. Angus's trouble hasn't been diagnosed yet, so I can't say what kind of surgery he'd have to undergo—if any. But I can promise you one thing: every care will be taken to ensure that he's returned to you safe and in good health.'

'That's a great comfort,' sighed Moira.

'And, Moira. . .'

'Yes?'

'You really do have an awful lot to thank your mother for. Her love for Angus—and for you—was her only motive for insisting you took Angus to the doctor.'

Moira's eyes filled with tears. 'Oh, I know that fine. It's just that I've been so worried. I've known for some time that something was wrong, you see, but Ian said I was babying Angus too much—making a cissy out of him. Oh, it's not that he doesn't love the wee boy—just that he wants him to grow up tough and manly.'

'Which he can't if he isn't well,' Corrie pointed out.

'He realises that now. But it's been a strain on our marriage,' Moira confessed. 'That and worrying about Angus has made me snappy, and I'm afraid Mum has been the one I've taken it out on. Especially when she kept fussing about the one thing I was already out of my mind with worry over.'

Corrie smiled. 'I'm sure she understands. Once Angus has seen the consultant you'll all feel better.'

'I hope so,' Moira sighed. 'Oh, I do hope so. But I feel better already, just with talking to you.

Corrie picked up Kathy, Moira and tiny, fair-haired Angus in the Rover next morning at eight o'clock. The drive into Inverness was smooth and uneventful and they arrived at the hospital in good time for Angus's appointment. Luckily they weren't kept waiting too long. Moira asked if Corrie would go in with her when she saw the consultant.

'You'll understand what he says better than I will,' she said nervously.

As it turned out, it was the consultant's registrar who was taking the clinic that morning. He was a studious-looking young man with dark hair and horn-rimmed glasses. He introduced himself as Gerald Jameson and explained that the senior consultant had been called to an emergency in the theatre. To Corrie's embarrassment, Kathy introduced her to the young surgeon, telling him proudly that she had been a theatre sister in one of the big London hospitals. He smiled.

'Then I shall have to watch my Ps and Qs, shan't I?' he said with the ghost of a wink at Corrie. 'These theatre sisters can really put you in your place, you know!'

He examined Angus carefully and then sent for a nurse to take him and Moira along for tests. When they had gone he looked at Corrie.

'I dare say you've probably formed your own opinion,' he said. 'It's almost certainly a stenosis.'

'A faulty valve. That's what Dr Forbes, our GP, thought,' Corrie agreed.

The registrar looked at William's letter on the desk in front of him. 'Yes, so I see.' He smiled. 'I know William quite well—we trained together. Give him my best when you see him, won't you?'

'I will. So you think Angus will be fine?'

'Oh, yes. A valvotomy should prove completely successful.'

'Can it be done here, or will he need to go to one of the larger hospitals?' Corrie asked.

'Oh no, we can cope with that here. We have an experienced cardiologist joining our team next week, to help us set up our own cardiac unit. We'll be able to do much more advanced heart surgery then.'

'That's marvellous!' Corrie smiled. 'It would have

been expensive and difficult for Moira to travel down to London with Angus and stay with him there.'

Gerald Jameson walked to the door with her. 'I'll let William know as soon as I can get the little fellow a bed. I'll make it as soon as I can,' he promised. 'The sooner these things are done for a child of that age, the better. The mother looked as though the strain is getting to her too.'

The tests confirmed that the initial diagnosis was correct, and Moira was told the result before they left the hospital. On the drive back to Glencarron the atmosphere was noticeably lighter. Clearly it was a relief to know that Angus's condition could be put right, and the prospect of the operation seemed less frightening now. Corrie explained to them in simple terms what would be done.

'The little flap of skin at the opening of the artery is called a valve. It allows the blood through to the heart and prevents it from flowing back. If the valve is faulty, not enough blood gets through to the lungs, so it becomes starved of oxygen. The surgeon will repair the valve and then it will work as it should.'

'Who would have thought that a wee flap of skin could cause so much trouble?' Kathy said wonderingly. 'So it isn't a complicated operation, then?'

'It's still heart surgery, Mother,' Moira said anxiously. 'Isn't it, Corrie?'

'That's right. And as such it needs the greatest of skill,' Corrie warned. 'Angus will go into Intensive Care as soon as he comes out of the theatre and stay there for at least the first twenty-four hours, so that he can be carefully monitored. But the good news is

that the operation can be done here, and Mr Jameson
has promised not to keep you waiting too long either.'

It was quite late by the time Corrie had dropped
off the little family and returned to Glencoe House.
Sheila was eagerly awaiting news of the day's excur-
sion, and Corrie told her everything that had taken
place over a cup of tea. Soon after that it was time for
them to get ready to go to dinner with Walter and
William.

The Forbes family had lived at Duncairn Lodge, the
spacious granite house on the edge of the town, ever
since Dr Walter's grandfather had bought the practice
at the turn of the century. In those days Glencarron
had been little more than a fishing village, and the
surgery had been built on to the house soon after the
war when the population had begun to increase. But
with the discovery of oil further along the coast, the
fishing trade had diminished, and with it the population. Corrie hadn't been in the house for years, but
she remembered it the moment Walter opened the
door to them. The oak-panelled hall with its red
Turkey rugs and the smell of lavender wax polish
brought back memories of the days when she and her
father had first come to Glencarron.

When Walter ushered them into the airy sitting-
room at the back of the house the windows were open
on to the walled garden that had been her special
delight as a child. Standing by them, she breathed in
the scent coming from the profusion of pink roses
climbing the wall just outside.

'Mmm, how lovely! I remember those roses. Dad
and I had no garden of our own and I used to love to

come here to play.' She looked round. 'Where's William?'

'He had a call to make,' Walter told her. 'He'll be back soon, though—at least I hope so. Mrs Greig won't thank him to keep her good dinner waiting.' He crossed the room to a corner cabinet and took out a decanter. 'Sherry?'

Corrie shook her head. 'I won't, if you don't mind, Uncle Walt—I'm driving, but I'd love a glass of wine with my dinner.' She put her hand on the handle of the French window. 'May I have a wander round the garden?'

'Of course, my dear. Help yourself.'

She found it all just as she remembered. The long lawn, ending in a wild tangle of shrubbery where a child could play at jungles. Beyond that, the kitchen garden where fat raspberries and juicy golden gooseberries grew. Many a richly deserved tummyache had been initiated here, she remembered with a smile. Honeysuckle and clematis climbed the walls, filling the summer evening with warm heady fragrance. Corrie closed her eyes and stood breathing it in for a moment, nostalgic with memories of her father and a happy childhood.

'The swing is still there. Did you see it?'

She opened her eyes with a start to find William standing beside her. 'Oh, hello—no, I didn't look.'

He took her hand. 'Come on, I'll show you.'

At the bottom of the kitchen garden stood an ancient apple tree, its branches thick and gnarled. It hadn't borne fruit for many a year, but from one of the stouter branches a homemade swing hung on two thick ropes.

'Go on, have a go. I'll push you,' William invited with a grin.

Corrie shook her head. 'No, thanks. I remember falling off once when you refused to stop pushing me and I went too high,' she reminded him. 'You used to jump out of the bushes at me too, pretending to be a Red Indian. You had a homemade bow and arrow and you used to paint your face and frighten me half to death.'

'I promise not to do that any more,' William said gravely. 'Anyway, I got into terrible trouble over that bow. I'd pinched the elastic out of Mrs Greig's best pink thermal bloomers to make it. I stole them off the washing line. Dad gave me a good hiding.'

Corrie giggled. 'You really were a little horror, weren't you?'

He put his hand over his heart. 'I'm a reformed character. I've seen the error of all my wicked ways, I promise.' He took her arm. 'Shall we start walking back? I don't want to incur Mrs Greig's wrath again, and I think her dinner might be spoiling.'

As they walked back she told him about her trip to the hospital with Angus and about meeting his friend Gerald Jameson.

'I know—I've already spoken to Gerry on the phone. They'll be taking Angus in a week tomorrow,' he told her.

'So soon?'

'That's right.' He glanced at her. 'Gerry might have told you that they're opening their own cardiac unit soon and they have a senior consultant coming up to set it up for them. Gerry is a recent appointment too, so they're not short of staff at the moment.'

'It'll be a big relief to Kathy and Angus's parents.'

'It certainly will.'

'Was your house call an emergency?' she asked.

'It wasn't really a house call. I went to see Gavin McLeod. I hoped I might get him to help old Morag out.'

'What did he say?' asked Corrie.

William sighed. 'Much the same as before. He wrapped it up tactfully in yards of that oily charm of his, but what it comes down to is that he thinks she's a damned nuisance and should be put away.'

Corrie turned to him. '*I'll* go and see him,' she said impulsively.

He stared at her, one eyebrow raised in amusement. '*You*? What do you think you can do?'

She thrust out her chin. 'It is just possible, *Wullie Forbes*, that I can be a little more persuasive than you.'

He laughed. 'Ah, I see, you're planning to seduce him into giving way, are you?'

She blushed. 'Don't be so sexist! There are other weapons a woman can use, you know.'

He picked up her hand and pulled it through his arm. 'None as interesting or as much fun, though, don't you agree?' He bent to kiss her cheek. 'Though in Gavin's case I'm relieved to hear that you don't intend to use your feminine wiles,' he whispered. 'I could get seriously jealous.'

Mrs Greig, the Forbeses' housekeeper, produced a delicious meal. Under Dr Walter's strict instructions she had adhered carefully to Sheila's diet, producing food that was healthy yet satisfying, with no intolerable temptations for Sheila. After they had eaten Walter suggested a game of backgammon.

'What are you young people going to do?' he asked William. 'Join us, or have you something else planned?'

'I'd rather like to see the surgery,' Corrie said. 'I haven't been in it since Dad died, and I dare say you've made some improvements since then.'

William looked pleased. 'Of course—I'd love to show you. We've installed a new computer system now. I never get tired of showing it off.'

The door connecting the house to the surgery led straight into the reception area, and Corrie stood looking around her with interest. She had been right in assuming that changes had been made. It was brightly decorated in pastel colours and a smart new reception desk stood in one corner, a hatch connecting it to the dispensary behind.

'We have a lot more room now that we don't have to store all those bulky records,' William told her. 'Wonderful, isn't it? Notes for more than a hundred patients on one small disk.'

William had adopted the room that had been her father's surgery, but again it had been completely renovated. Corrie found new bright décor and carpet. Gone was the heavy oak bookcase full of medical tomes, and in its place a neat cabinet with sliding glass doors, storing up-to-date reference books. Dr Ashley's heavy antique desk had been replaced by a modern one large enough to accommodate the neat computer keyboard and VDU.

'The new system must cut down the need for staff. How many do you employ these days?' Corrie asked.

'Mrs Hamilton, our dispenser, is still with us. I expect you remember her. And I have a part-time receptionist. Dad helps out a bit, manning the telephone in the afternoons, when he isn't counselling, and taking the odd surgery for me in an emergency. Mrs Greig took calls till her hearing began to fail. Now we have an answerphone.' William grinned boyishly. 'Did I tell you I'm getting a car phone? That'll be a big help. But what I could *really* do with is a practice nurse. She'd be able to take a lot of the routine work off my shoulders and leave me free for the more serious cases.'

'Can't you find one?' asked Corrie.

He shook his head. 'All the young girls who go into nursing want jobs with plenty of social life when they qualify. They go off to nurse in the large city hospitals. No, practice nursing is more for the woman returning to work after bringing up a family—at least, in places like this.'

'And there aren't any of those in Glencarron?'

'Seems not.' He looked at her and she knew from the wicked look in his eyes that he was about to say something embarrassing. She was right.

'Maybe when you've finished having all those bairns that Morag saw in your hand, you'd like the job,' he said, lifting an eyebrow at her.

'I think Morag has her wires crossed somewhere,' said Corrie, refusing to rise to the bait. 'I have no plans for marriage, bairns— *or* practice nursing. And anyhow, I have a job at the moment.'

He shrugged. 'Ah well, I dare say you'd find it too boring anyway. We must all seem like country gobbins to you up here in the Highlands. You must be struggling not to laugh at me, getting all excited about computers and car phones, when to you they're just everyday necessities.'

There was an acid sharpness in his tone that she didn't quite understand. 'That's not true at all, William.' She looked at her watch and turned away. 'Maybe we should be getting back. Sheila isn't used to late nights and——' She broke off as he grasped her arm and pulled her round to face him again.

'Don't walk away from me, Corrie. Sheila's fine. You've done a great job on her. She's a different woman since you've been looking after her.'

'It's not just me. You keep an eye on her too. Then there's Christie and your father. . .'

'What if you'd succeeded so well that you'd worked yourself out of a job? What would you do if you found she didn't need you any more?'

Corrie frowned. 'Do you know something I don't know?'

'I might.'

For a moment they looked into each other's eyes, Corrie's troubled, William's enigmatic. Then he asked, 'Are you still hankering for London, and for—the life you left behind?'

'No,' she said truthfully.

'But you do still think about it?'

'Yes, of course I do. It isn't possible to shrug off things that played a major part in one's life just like that.'

'No, of course it isn't—I know that.' He looked at her for a long moment, then suddenly, 'Would you marry me, if I were to ask you?'

Corrie felt herself flush hotly. 'Don't be absurd, William. Shall we go back?'

But he held her arm fast. 'You might at least answer.'

'Answer? As it was a hypothetical question I hardly think it needs or deserves one, William.'

'All right, then, I'll make it a definite question. Will you marry me, Corrie?'

For a moment it was as though time stopped as they stared at each other, then Corrie said, 'Well, since you ask—no.'

'Why not?'

'Give me one good reason why I should?'

His expression relaxed a little. 'Well, if you were to say yes I'd assume it might be because you loved me.'

'Precisely. See what I mean?'

He grinned. 'You wouldn't be getting your own back for all those childhood pranks, by any chance?'

'Of course I am.' She laughed, feeling relief wash over her. 'A frog in the wellie is worth a good firm jilting any day.'

He sighed with mock desolation. 'Ah, I might have known my sins would catch up with me one day.' Before she had a chance to resist he drew her close and kissed her hard till she had hardly any breath left. When they drew apart he looked down at her.

'I shall ask you just once more, Corrie. No, not now—later. But I warn you, that'll be the last time—the very last. So you'd better think carefully about it between now and then.'

And although his mouth smiled at her, his eyes were in deadly earnest.

CHAPTER EIGHT

GLENCARRON CASTLE stood on a small island on the loch. At one time it had been attainable only by boat, so that the loch took the place of a moat in defending it. But a little over a hundred years ago a previous laird had built a sturdy stone bridge across from the shore, making access much easier.

Sheila, who was totally in favour of Corrie's visit, had lent her the Rover for the afternoon. Corrie had telephoned to make the appointment the previous day, after they had dined with William and his father. She had felt very brave at the time, feeling she had right on her side, but now, standing looking across at the grey stone castle, forbidding against a backcloth of storm-darkened sky, she was not quite as confident.

Leaving the car on the shore, she walked across the bridge and stood before the massive front door, tugging hard at the large iron ring that hung on a chain beside it. The sound of the bell jangled and echoed through the thick stone walls, reminding her shudderingly of something out of a horror film. But the young woman who answered it looked pleasant and normal enough in her cheerful print overall.

'Miss Ashley?' she smiled. 'Come away in. The Laird is expecting you. He's in the library just along here, if you'll follow me.'

Corrie followed her through the huge hallway, from the centre of which climbed an impressive carved staircase. In the massive fireplace a log fire burned. Above it hung a life-size portrait of a fearsome-looking man in Highland battle dress complete with bonnet and crested shield.

'My ancestor, Alasdair McLeod. He fell commanding his men at Culloden.' Gavin McLeod stood in the library doorway. He looked relaxed in riding breeches and a polo-necked sweater. 'Come in, Miss Ashley. Will you take a cup of tea with me?'

'No, thank you. I won't take up too much of your time,' Corrie said. She was determined not to be put at a disadvantage by what William had called Gavin's 'oily charm'.

Another wood fire burned in the library fireplace, and Gavin went to stand beside it. 'It feels cold even in the height of summer,' he explained. 'The walls are too thick to let in the temperatures outside, which is just as well in the winter. But there are few days when we don't need a fire.' He indicated a chair to her. 'Please be seated. Now, what can I do for you?'

Corrie came straight to the point. 'I've come to ask you to help old Morag Kincaid.'

He sighed, an expression of dismay crossing his face. 'Ah, yes.'

'Don't you think that as Laird you have some small duty by her?' she asked directly.

He turned to face her. 'You think that the old woman is a case for charity?'

'No. I'm quite sure she wouldn't accept charity.'

'Well, then?'

'But she is poor and ill, and you're her landlord,' Corrie pressed. 'Dr Forbes is quite concerned about her.'

He smiled indolently. 'I'm fully aware of the doctor's views. Did he send you here to plead his cause?'

Corrie flushed angrily. 'Of course he didn't! I came of my own accord.'

'May I ask what your interest is?' he queried.

'I feel that Morag deserves a little comfort in her old age. All her life she's asked for nothing and done what she felt she was put here on earth for—tending wild creatures.'

'If you'll forgive me, Miss Ashley, your view of her seems rather idealised. I don't know about doing what she was put on earth for. I do know that she's lived on McLeod land rent-free for nigh on the last fifty years, and if you think I should be grateful to her for tending sick vermin to kill my farmers' lambs and eat their meagre crops. . .'

'I'm not here to argue with you, Mr McLeod. I just think you might do some small thing to help Morag, if only as—as a human being.'

He smiled cynically. 'I see. Well, I'm flattered that at least you see me as human. So what do you suggest?'

'If you could just repair her croft so that it was habitable—mend the roof to keep out the damp. And do something about that awful earth floor.'

'Perhaps you'd like me to install central heating? What about a swimming pool while we're about it?' Gavin threw up his hands impatiently. 'Miss Ashley, do you have any idea what it costs to keep up this heap of crumbling grandeur?'

'Surely the repair of one small croft. . .'

'Over the generations death duties and capital transfer tax have almost crippled my family,' Gavin went on. 'Most of the land I own is moorland. It isn't productive, so no one wants to buy it. My few tenant farmers are hardly able to make ends meet. I could sell the grouse moor and castle to a wealthy Arab or a Texan oil millionaire and go and live a life of luxury in the South of France, but I think the people of Glencarron might feel slightly let down if I did that, don't you?' Taken aback by his vehemence, Corrie shook her head. 'So my only, my *last* resort, is to try to make some money out of the tourist trade. I'm opening the castle to the public this year—on a residential basis; strictly selective, of course. I'm not planning to erect a neon sign or turn the gun-room into a burger bar. Another of my plans is to convert the crofts—there are twelve of them—into time-share holiday cottages. I don't *want* to do it, Miss Ashley. I'd much prefer to have my home to myself like anyone else. But it's that or go under.'

'But couldn't you let Morag stay on?' pleaded Corrie. 'She's very old. She can't have so many more years left.'

'Neither will this estate if I don't do something, and do it quickly.' He sighed deeply and sat down opposite her. 'I take it *you* get along with her?'

'Well—yes,' she agreed.

'I hope you realise how rare that is. She's not exactly renowned for her hospitality. Not to put too fine a point on it, Miss Ashley, she's as wild as the animals she's so fond of.'

'I know she can be a little—eccentric,' Corrie admitted.

He gave a bark of mirthless laughter. 'That's the understatement of the century! She's got an old shotgun at the croft and she isn't afraid of using it. Even I have had to run for my life more than once, and I'm supposed to be her landlord!' He rose again to walk to the fireplace. 'Be realistic—if she doesn't get on with the local people, can you see her fitting in with holidaymakers?'

'Well, I suppose not, but. . .'

Gavin shook his head. 'Look, I'm sorry, Miss Ashley, but that old woman stands between me and the secure future of Glencarron Castle. If she's ill, I'm sorry, but I truly believe that if that's the case then the best place for her is an old people's home or a hospital. Even your doctor friend had to admit that was true.'

'It would kill her,' Corrie said bleakly.

He turned to look at her levelly. 'To be brutally frank, maybe that would be best for everyone concerned,' he said.

Corrie got to her feet. 'I don't have to ask if that's your last word, Mr McLeod,' she said. 'Thank you for giving me your time. Good afternoon.'

He walked to the door with her. 'I'm sorry I can't help, Miss Ashley,' he said. 'And I admire you for standing up for the old girl. But I hope I've made you see my point.'

She turned to look at him. In her heart she was angry at what seemed his hard attitude, but the practical side of her saw that if what he had told her was true, his situation precluded sentimentality.

'I see it, Mr McLeod,' she said quietly. 'I only hope Morag will.'

* * *

William called in after surgery that evening to ask how the visit to the castle had gone, and Corrie was forced to admit that she had done no better than he had.

'The trouble is, I can see his point,' she said. 'He hasn't actually said he's going to evict Morag, but he hasn't said he won't either.'

'He told me he'd leave the work on her croft till last,' William told her. 'And I'm very much afraid I'm the one who'll have to break the news to her.'

'Poor William!' Corrie looked at him with genuine sympathy, knowing the compassion he felt for the old woman. 'I'll go with you when the time comes, if you like.'

He smiled. 'Thanks, Corrie. I might take you up on that. In the meantime I'll have to set about looking for somewhere suitable for her.'

Sheila shook her head. 'I can't see her taking kindly to being cooped up in a centrally heated room all day and told what to do, after being free to wander the moor and mountain. Suppose she digs her heels in— refuses to leave till the bulldozers arrive?'

William shuddered. 'That's something I'm trying not to think about. We'll meet that problem when we come to it.' He looked at Corrie. 'Speaking of which, I wanted to ask you both a favour. When Moira takes Angus into hospital on Monday would you go with her, Corrie?' He looked from one to the other. 'I know it means Sheila doing without you for a couple of days, but. . .'

'A *couple* of days?' Corrie raised her eyebrows at him.

'Yes—I was coming to that. She's bound to be

anxious while he's in theatre, so it would be nice for her to have company—just till it's all over.'

'What about Kathy? Surely Moira would rather have her own mother with her?'

William shook his head. 'As a matter of fact I've advised against that. Kathy tends to fuss. It's natural, of course, but Moira's nerves are pretty raw and she'd be better off with someone who isn't so closely involved. As a matter of fact, it was her own suggestion, though she didn't like to ask you herself. She likes and trusts you, Corrie. And I do feel you'd be a calming influence on her.' He looked at Sheila. 'Can you manage without her for a couple of days? I wouldn't ask if I didn't feel it was important.'

'Of course I can manage,' said Sheila. 'After all, I dare say Corrie will be getting restless before long. I shall have to learn to do without her some time, shan't I?'

'Well, after that I can hardly refuse, can I?' Corrie smiled as they both looked at her. 'Though you're quite wrong—I'm not at all restless. I'm happy to stay here as long as you want me, Sheila.'

In the silence that followed Corrie sensed a slight discomfort in the atmosphere. She thought she saw a quick conspiratorial glance pass between William and Sheila. Then William said, 'How about a walk by the loch?'

'That's right, get some fresh air before bedtime,' added Sheila.

Corrie looked out of the window. 'It looks as though the storm that's been threatening all day is about to break.'

'We won't go far.' William stood up and held out his hand.

Did he want to see her privately? Was there something Sheila had asked him to tell her? Something about the look in his eyes told her this was so, and that it was important. With a leaden feeling in her heart she rose. 'All right, I'll get an anorak.'

They walked along the shore in silence for a while. The loch was strangely still and the mountains were shrouded in mist as the heavy storm clouds hung low over them. Sensing her feeling of apprehension, William felt for her hand and squeezed it.

'There's something I think you should know.'

'I thought there might be.' She looked up at him. 'You'd better tell me.'

'Well, prepare yourself for a surprise, if not a shock.'

Corrie shot him an impatient glance. 'Oh, *William*! Are you going to tell me, or aren't you?'

'Dad has asked Sheila to marry him.'

She stopped walking to stare at him. It was the last thing she had expected. 'Has she accepted?' she asked.

He shrugged. 'Not yet, but I think she will. They've always been good friends. He's extremely fond of her, and I think he'd like to be closer to help her now that she really needs someone.'

Corrie felt a lump rise in her throat. 'Dear Uncle Walt! How typical of him!'

'I happen to think they'd make each other very happy,' William said. 'Sheila has taken to the regimen we've set her very well and there's no reason why she shouldn't lead a full and happy life for a good many years. As a doctor, Dad is perfectly aware of the prognosis. He knows what he's letting himself in for. It really is the ideal arrangement, when you think about it.'

After the initial surprise Corrie's mind was working fast. All those hints about her being restless and bored in the Highlands—wanting to leave soon. And William's proposal—had it been his way of offering her an alternative? Had he seen it as a good way of getting the practice nurse he so badly needed? Immediately she was ashamed of the thought. William wasn't devious. It was much more likely that he saw it as a practical idea; an *ideal arrangement*, was the phrase he'd used. Aloud she said, 'Yes, I suppose it is. I'd better start looking for another job, then, hadn't I?'

'I thought I'd warn you,' said William. 'Sheila was too embarrassed to tell you herself. She asked me to break the ice, as it were.'

'Thanks. I knew this was only a temporary job when I took it.'

'Corrie,' he stopped walking, 'there's no need for you to leave Glencarron if you don't want to.'

'I know.' She felt her heartbeat quicken as the green eyes looked into hers. Suddenly she longed for the reassurance of his arms around her. If he were to kiss her now, say he loved her—if she could be *sure* he meant it. Yet if he did. . . She pushed the tortured thoughts to the back of her mind and tore her eyes away from his, beginning to walk back towards the house. A sudden heavy raindrop splashed coldly against her face, quickly followed by another, and a moment later the smooth surface of the loch was dimpled with fast-falling rain. A distant rumble of thunder stirred the turgid air. William turned up his collar and grasped her hand.

'Come on—run for it!'

Sheila had gone to bed when they got back to the house, and William left as soon as he had delivered Corrie to the door, saying there was a patient he wanted to look in on before turning in.

Corrie lay sleepless for a long time after she was in bed, kept awake by the thunder that rolled up and down the glen like a trapped tiger, and the livid flashes of lightning that lit the room with silver-blue light. But even if it had been a calm night she would not have slept. Once, not so many weeks ago, it had been thoughts of Hugh that filled her mind and tugged painfully at her heart in those last waking moments. Now when she closed her eyes it was William she saw—his broad shoulders and the sun shining on the coppery hair, the laughing green eyes and the strong, capable hands. She tried to remember when this change had taken place, but she couldn't. It had happened almost without her noticing. '*I can't have fallen in love with him, can I?*' she asked herself aloud. But even as she said it she knew she must have. All the signs were there: the sudden quickening of her pulse when he came into the room, the melting sensation when he took her in his arms. And his kiss. . . *No.* She wouldn't think about his kiss. Instead she asked herself what life as William's wife would be like. Running the practice together, living together in the lovely old granite house she had always loved. Would it feel like being buried alive? She smiled to herself, suddenly remembering old Morag's prophecy:

A braw laddie who'll mak' ye a fine man an' gie ye bonny bairns. At the time she had been appalled and embarrassed at the idea. Now suddenly it seemed an idyllic prospect.

She shook the romantic notion from her mind and punched her pillow impatiently, reminding herself firmly that for William it would be a rebound love. She would be second best, and she didn't intend to be second best for anyone. Besides, could she really be sure that memories of Hugh were completely erased? Was it still too soon? No. If Sheila made up her mind to marry Dr Walter she would return to London and get another job. It shouldn't be too difficult to start again. After all, she had done it before. She closed her eyes, willing sleep to come to her rescue, turning her mind away from the dismay that threatened to overwhelm her.

It was at breakfast next morning that Sheila finally brought up the subject.

'Corrie, did William tell you my news last night?'

Corrie looked up. 'About Uncle Walt, you mean?'

'Yes.'

'What did you think? That we must be a pair of dotty old fools to even contemplate marriage, I dare say.'

Suddenly Corrie saw why Sheila hadn't wanted to tell her herself—she'd been too embarrassed. 'Of course I don't think that, Sheila,' she said. 'I think it's lovely—and *very* romantic!'

'He's asked me so many times over the years,' Sheila said, 'so I know it isn't just that he feels sorry for me. At first I said no because I wanted my independence, so when I contracted MS it seemed unfair to suddenly say yes; like making a convenience of him.'

'I'm sure Uncle Walt doesn't see it that way,' Corrie assured her.

'No. I'm so lucky to have such a dear man, willing to share his life with me.' Sheila smiled at Corrie. 'Lucky to have found you too. It's only because you've helped me so much in the management of my illness that I feel able to accept Walter's offer. I'd have hated to be a drag on him. But now that I feel so much better I feel I'll be able to contribute at least a little to our partnership.'

'Well, I wish you both all the best of good luck,' Corrie said. 'And now of course I shall have to think about looking for another job.'

Sheila's face fell. 'Oh! But I thought. . .' She trailed off, and Corrie said, 'You thought—what?'

'Oh, nothing. Just that there might have been something here in Glencarron for you. We've all grown so fond of you, and so used to having you around. We'll miss you. William. . .' She hesitated, and Corrie looked at her.

'Yes—William?'

'He needs a nurse for the practice, I do know that. I dare say your skills would be wasted on a job of that kind, though. It wouldn't be fair to ask you to take it just because we like having you here, would it?'

Corrie was saved from replying to this when the telephone in the hall suddenly rang. She got up from the breakfast table. 'I'll get it.'

William's voice at the other end of the line sounded

urgent. 'Corrie, I'm at Kirsty McEwan's house. She called me out to her father an hour ago.'

'Is he ill?' she asked.

'I'm afraid he's in a coma. Look, when the ambulance arrives I want to go with him to the hospital, but I can't leave Kirsty here alone—she's naturally very upset. Could you possibly drive over and stay with her?'

'Of course. I'm sure Sheila won't mind, but wouldn't her neighbour come in?'

William lowered his voice. 'I don't want to involve anyone else. There are—complications.'

'What kind of complications?' queried Corrie.

'I can't talk about it on the telephone, but I'm worried about him, which is why I want to go with him in the ambulance.'

'I'll be with you as soon as I can.'

He gave her directions for finding Kirsty's house and then rang off.

The McEwans lived in a small house quite close to the quay. It was easy to spot as an ambulance stood outside when Corrie drew up, its rear doors open. William was supervising the removal of the unconscious patient to the waiting vehicle. He looked relieved when he saw her.

'Thanks for coming so quickly, Corrie,' he said. 'Kirsty's through in the kitchen.'

'I'll go to her.' She glanced at the ashen face of the man on the trolley-bed. 'How is he?'

William shook his head. 'Not good. Kirsty will tell you the details. Tell her I'll be in touch by phone as soon as I know anything.' He climbed into the ambulance as the men slid the trolley into position and secured it. The doors were closed and the vehicle set off.

Kirsty walked through the narrow hallway and pushed open the door at the end. Kirsty sat at the kitchen table, her eyes red and a crumpled handkerchief tightly squeezed in her hand.

'Kirsty.' Corrie laid a hand on the girl's shoulder. 'Can I do anything for you, love? Shall I make us a coffee or some tea?'

The other girl got to her feet and suddenly threw herself into Corrie's arms, sobbing, 'Oh, Corrie, he did it for me. It's all my fault!'

Corrie held the sobbing girl for a moment, then she asked gently, 'Did what? What did he do? Tell me.'

Kirsty pulled a piece of notepaper out of her pocket and spread it out on the table. 'I found this on the table by his bed when I went to wake him this morning,' she said. 'In it he says he took an overdose of his tablets, so that I could be free to live the kind of life I deserve.'

Corrie read the brief note while Kirsty wept quietly into the sodden handkerchief. The handwriting was crabbed and the wording was somewhat garbled, but the meaning was clear enough. John McEwan had decided to end his life because he felt he was a burden on his daughter. She slipped an arm round the girl's shoulders, wondering what she could possibly do or say to help.

'I feel so guilty,' Kirsty sobbed. 'It all started when I met Brian again. We've known each other all our lives, but we've been seeing each other regularly since the Laird's birthday dance. A week ago Brian asked me to marry him, but I said I couldn't while Dad was alive. Dad had been very awkward since I'd met Brian again—I think he could see the way things were. Maybe it made him feel insecure, as though he was afraid I might leave him, even though I kept trying to reassure him. Anyway, we had a row, and I said—I told him I'd turned Brian down, given up everything for him.' She swallowed hard. 'Oh, Corrie, I said some awful, cruel things to him. All the feelings of resentment I'd pushed down for years just erupted like a volcano. If *only* I hadn't said them!'

'You mustn't take all the blame on to yourself. You're human like the rest of us,' Corrie told her gently.

Kirsty shook her head. 'I keep seeing his face. Oh, Corrie, I wouldn't have hurt Dad for the world. If *only* he'd just talked to me—told me about his fears.'

'Does Brian know what's happened?' Corrie asked.

Kirsty shook her head. 'The last time we met I told him I couldn't see him any more.'

'But this is different. I'm sure he'd want to be with you. Can I get in touch with him? Where does he work?'

Kirsty blew her nose. 'He's at home on holiday this week. It was the holiday plans that brought things to a head—he'd asked me to go away with him. Oh, Corrie, I wanted so *much* to go. I felt so torn between him and Dad.'

'You should have asked Dr William,' Corrie told her. 'Your father could have gone into hospital just for a week.' She pressed Kirsty's hand. 'Look, go and ring Brian while I make the coffee. And try not to feel so guilty. Your father's a sick man, I dare say he gets depressed and weary of his illness. If he intended to do this thing, then it wouldn't only have been on your account.' She stood up and went to fill the kettle. 'Off you go and make that call. I'm going to make us some coffee. Do you have any brandy in the house?'

Kirsty came back from making the call looking calmer. Shocked at her news, Brian had promised to come over to the house at once. Corrie was in the McEwans' sitting-room ten minutes later, looking for the brandy in the sideboard cupboard, when the telephone rang. She snatched up the receiver quickly.

'Hello. Corinne Ashley speaking.'

'Oh, Corrie, I'm glad it's you. I'm afraid it's bad news. John McEwan died ten minutes ago.'

'Oh, William, I'm so sorry. Do you want me to break the news to Kirsty?'

'Could you? I'm sorry to give you such an awful job. But there is one thing you can tell her. He didn't die of an overdose.'

'He didn't? Then what?' she asked.

'I don't know. We'll have to wait for the PM. But the washout he had on admittance revealed nothing it shouldn't. Maybe he meant to do it but didn't have time. But at least it will be a relief to Kirsty.'

'I'll tell her,' said Corrie.

Kirsty took the news bravely, and surprisingly well, as though she had been expecting it. And the news that her father's death had been natural after all was clearly a relief. Corrie was just making a second cup of coffee when the door opened and Brian stood on the threshold. His face was pale, but his eyes held love and concern for Kirsty. Corrie quietly put the two mugs of coffee on the table and patted the girl on the shoulder.

'I'll go, then,' she said with a smile at the young man. 'You're in good hands now, but you know where I am if you need me.'

As she started the Rover and headed back to Glencoe House she reflected that at least Kirsty wasn't alone in her grief. In fact, if the look in Brian's eyes was anything to go by, she wouldn't have to face life alone in the future either.

On Sunday evening there was a small dinner party at Glencoe House to celebrate Sheila's and Dr Walter's engagement. Kathy had come in specially to cook for them. It was, as she said, her engagement present to the happy couple. She also told Corrie while they were in the kitchen together that it helped take her mind off her grandson's operation.

'I'm glad you're going with Moira,' she said. 'I'd have been no use to her—I get too emotional. I realise that. And I'm sure you'll be a comfort to her. You're always so calm.'

Corrie smiled wryly to herself. 'Calm' was hardly the word she'd have used if she'd been asked to describe herself.

After dinner William offered to drive Kathy home. He looked at Corrie.

'Coming with me for the ride? We came in Dad's car, so there's plenty of room.'

She stood up. It occurred to her that Sheila and Uncle Walt might like to have a little time alone together on their engagement evening. 'Yes. I'll just get a coat,' she said.

When they had seen Kathy safely inside her cottage

William looked at Corrie. 'How about a glass of wine at the Gordon Arms?'

She smiled. 'That sounds nice.'

As they sat before the log fire in the cosy bar William raised his glass. 'Here's to the future Dr and Mrs Forbes.'

Corrie lifted her glass to clink it against his. 'Sheila and Uncle Walt.'

He looked at her quizzically. 'Shall we drink to ourselves too?'

She shrugged. 'Why not?'

'To the future?'

'If you like.'

'And what does the future hold for you, Corrie? Have you decided what you'll do?'

She avoided his eyes, looking into her glass. 'Not yet, except that I don't think I shall be staying here.'

'Maybe you could make some enquiries when you're up at the hospital tomorrow. I dare say they'd snap up an experienced theatre sister like you. It isn't London, but it's bound to be more exciting than Glencarron.'

There was a lump in Corrie's throat as she looked at him. Talking about leaving, finding another job, made it seem so final somehow. Part of her longed to reach for his hand, beg him to ask her to stay. But another part of her still held back, still felt unsure.

'You know that you belong here, don't you, Corrie?' he said quietly. 'Your roots are here, even though it's not where you were born. Something will always call you back.'

'Perhaps,' she said.

He drained his glass. 'I think you suspect that when

you get back inside a hospital, feel that highly charged atmosphere, you'll itch to be back in the swim, part of the excitement—the life or death drama.' He looked up at her with a sudden heart-stopping directness. 'Or is it something—some*one* else that draws you back?' Before she could reply he took her hand. 'Let's get out of here,' he said, a rough edge to his voice. 'Dad will be waiting.'

He didn't speak on the short drive back, and when he drew the car up at the foot of the steps he turned to her.

'I won't come in. If you'll just tell Dad I'm waiting.'

She looked at him in surprise. 'Aren't you going to say goodnight to Sheila?'

'Make my apologies,' he said. 'Say it for me.'

She stared at him in dismay. 'William, what's the matter? Did I say something to. . .' He grasped her shoulders and pulled her to him, kissing her fiercely till her mouth felt bruised. She lifted her arms to put them round his neck, but he put her away from him abruptly. Holding both her hands, he looked into her eyes.

'Go in now, Corrie,' he commanded. 'I'll see you on Wednesday, when you get back from the hospital—perhaps.'

She stared at him, her heart aching with hurt bewilderment. He was deliberately shutting her out, and she was shocked at the feeling of despondency that overwhelmed her. Shaking her head helplessly, she turned to open the car door.

'Goodnight, William.'

The grey-green eyes looked into hers. 'Goodbye—Corrie.'

CHAPTER NINE

As Angus had to be at the hospital by ten o'clock the following morning Corrie was up early, packing her overnight bag with the few things she would need. Sheila came down in time to see her off. As they stood together at the front door Sheila said, 'Corrie, tell me to mind my own business if you like, but I have to ask. Did you and William have a row last night?'

'No. I think he was just tired. He works very hard.'

Sheila nodded. 'He certainly does. Now, if he had a wife to help him. . .' Corrie stopped her words with a look.

'Sheila, William might marry for convenience, I don't know. I do know that *I* never would. Maybe I'm an incurable romantic, but I happen to have this conviction that one should be in love.' The moment the words were out she realised how tactless they were. Feeling the colour warm her cheeks, she added quickly, 'Oh, I don't mean you and Uncle Walt, of course.'

Sheila laughed. 'My dear, of course you don't. He and I are past all that. Besides, we've both had romantic love once in our lives, and no one can ever repeat it—when it's right, that is. Believe me, I do know what you mean, though I do think that sometimes one can be too close to see things properly.' She looked thoughtful. 'What did you mean about William's marrying for convenience?'

Corrie shrugged. 'He had someone who was special once, did he? Fiona?'

Sheila frowned. 'If it's the same Fiona I met she certainly wasn't special to him in that way. He helped her through a bad patch, that's all.'

'Oh, but Uncle Walt said. . .'

Sheila smiled. 'Walter's a sentimental old silly sometimes. It was a bit of wishful thinking, because he wants William to marry and give him some grandchildren, that's all.' She looked at her watch. 'Now off you go, my dear. Mustn't keep poor Moira waiting. Maybe while you're away from us all you'll have time to think. Drive carefully, and come back to us safely on Wednesday.'

Little Angus was fretful on the journey. He clung to his mother begging her over and over not to leave him, and although she promised again and again to stay with him, he would not be consoled.

'Ian and I thought it best to prepare him for going into hospital,' Moira told Corrie. 'We explained as best one can to a child as young as he is. But I'm afraid it just seems to have scared him—made things worse.' She sighed. 'Oh, dear, I'll be so glad when it's all over.'

At the hospital the admittance procedure and the various routine tests seemed to take ages, with Angus whimpering fractiously and clinging to his mother. But at last they were free to go back to the ward and attempt to settle him. The children's ward was arranged in a series of small rooms with a cot or bed for the child and another for the mother. The wall that faced the corridor was made of glass so that nursing staff could keep a check on the patients, but with curtains that could be drawn by the mother for privacy.

'It's a lot nicer than I thought it would be,' said Moira.

'After the op Angus will be in the intensive care unit for a while,' Corrie warned. 'But he'll be sedated, so he won't fret too much that you aren't there with him all the time. After that you'll be able to help nurse him back here until he's discharged.'

The mention of the operation reminded Moira of why they were here, and her face drained of colour as she stood in the midst of her unpacking, a tiny pair of pyjamas in her hands. 'Oh, dear! Every time I think of it my stomach turns over,' she whispered.

Together they settled Angus in the playroom with some of the other small patients. The sight of all the toys made him forget his anxiety, though he still kept looking round at his mother for reassurance.

'What about you?' asked Moira. 'Don't you want to go and unpack your own things and setttle in?'

William had booked Corrie a room at a nearby hotel and she had not had time so far to go and check in. 'Well, if you're sure you'll be all right for a while,' she said, 'I would like to freshen up. If Angus will let you leave him for a while we could go to the hospital canteen later and have some lunch, but if you ask one of the nurses she'll show you where there's a drinks machine.'

Moira smiled. 'Of course. I'll be just fine. Take your time.'

The hotel William had booked was only across the road from the hospital. Corrie unpacked her overnight case and took a shower, then, after running a brush through her hair and applying a dash of lipstick, she went back to the hospital. Moira and Angus were not in the playroom and when she went along to their room she found the curtains drawn. Clearly the cardiac consultant had come to examine Angus. She took a seat in the corridor, but she didn't have long to wait before the curtains were drawn back by the ward sister. Corrie could see the consultant. He stood with his back to her, speaking to Moira, and now that the door was open she could hear his words.

'Try not to worry too much, Mrs Andrews. This time tomorrow it will be over, and all you'll have to do is look forward to the future.'

Her heart almost stopped beating. The voice was unmistakable, and so was the tall, grey-suited figure. Everything about him was so heart-stoppingly familiar—the way his hair grew, the way he held his head. For a second she felt panic-stricken. Her first instinct was to turn and run. Her heart hammered with a sickening dullness inside her chest. Slowly she stood up on legs that felt like jelly. Maybe if she were to walk quietly away now, no one would notice. It was at that very moment that he turned and caught sight of her.

'*Corrie!*' He stopped in his tracks, his eyes widening, totally oblivious of Sister's curious stare. 'What on earth are you doing here?'

'Hello, Hugh.'

In spite of the pounding of her heart and the way her mouth had dried, her voice sounded calm and steady.

'I'm here with Moira—Mrs Andrews, and Angus,'

she added in answer to his question. Acutely aware herself of the sister's appraising glance and Moira's curious look, she felt her colour rise.

'So you're the nurse who's kindly come to keep Mrs Andrews company? Well, well.' He turned back towards Moira. 'I'm sure you won't mind if I borrow your friend, will you, Mrs Andrews? We're old friends, and we're going to have a lot of catching up to do.'

Corrie saw that Hugh's charm had obviously been used to best advantage on Moira, who smiled and nodded encouragingly. 'Of course,' she said.

Before she could express her own views Corrie found herself swept firmly along the corridor and into the lift, Hugh's hand under her elbow. To her dismay they were the only occupants, and the moment the doors closed he turned to her.

'Where have you *been* these past months? I thought you would have kept in touch. No one seemed to have a clue where you'd gone. It was as though you'd vanished into thin air.'

She stared at him. 'You knew I was leaving, Hugh—and the reason. You never even asked me where I was going. I've been up here in Scotland, caring for an MS sufferer, who happens to be my old headmistress.'

He shook his head in disbelief. 'Wasn't that going over the top a bit? Burying yourself alive at the back of beyond just because we split up.'

'That wasn't my only reason.' She heard the defensive edge her voice had assumed and cut the sentence short. 'Anyway, why are you here?'

'Me? I'm only up here to set up this new cardiac unit. The minute it's up and running I shall be off.'

'I can imagine,' Corrie said drily.

He put his hands on her shoulders. 'Anyway, it's good to see you, Corrie. I've missed you.'

She stared at him. 'Really?'

'Well, haven't you missed me?'

She met his gaze levelly. 'How is Lucille? And the children?'

He winced. 'Ouch! I suppose I deserve that. Well, since you ask, the *children*, as you call them, are living independent lives now, in flats of their own. And Lucille and I split up a month ago.'

She was unaware that her mouth had dropped open in surprise. 'Oh—I'm sorry.'

He gave her a wry smile. 'Are you? I find that just a little hard to believe.' He raised an eyebrow at her. 'Don't you want to know why we split up?'

The lift came to a stop. As the doors opened Corrie stepped quickly out. 'It's really none of my business.'

He caught at her arm. 'Wait! You're going the wrong way.'

'Hugh. . .' she turned to face him '. . . I'm here to do a job. I haven't time to gossip with you, and anyway, I don't think we have anything to say to each other. If you'll excuse me I'll——'

'There's a coffee bar next door to the hospital,' he said. 'At least come and have a coffee with me.' He wasn't asking but telling her. With her arm firmly in his grasp she could either go with him or make a scene. She went with him, through the reception area, out through the swing doors and on to the forecourt, all the time hating herself for her lack of resolve.

In the coffee bar they faced each other across the plastic-topped table. Hugh stirred his coffee, watching her face carefully as he said, 'She found someone else.'

Corrie looked up. 'Sorry? Who did?'

'*Lucille*. She fell in love. Couldn't just have a little fling like any other bored housewife—oh, no, not Lucille. It was all or nothing.'

'You wouldn't understand that, would you, Hugh?'

He ignored her remark. 'So—are you reasonably content with life, then?'

She raised an eyebrow. 'Reasonably content?'

He shrugged. 'Well, you could hardly be deliriously happy, could you?'

'Without you, do you mean? As a matter of fact I have been—*am*—happy,' she said. 'Glencarron is where I grew up. I have a lot of friends there.'

He smiled. 'I never knew you came from this part of the world. Isn't that odd?'

'There's a great deal you never knew or wanted to know about me, Hugh,' she told him. 'And a lot that you'd never understand if you did.' She finished her coffee and stood up. 'I really do have to go now.'

He looked up at her. 'Have dinner with me this evening.'

'I can't,' she said firmly.

He rose slowly and stood facing her. 'I wish you would, Corrie.' He paused for a moment. 'How close are you to the child?'

'Angus? Not close at all. Moira's just a friend. Why?'

'Good. That's just as well.'

Her heart jerked. 'You haven't found something else, have you—some complication?'

'Where are you staying?' he asked.

'Across the road, at the Angel.'

'I'll pick you up at eight-thirty. I'd like to talk to you.'

'I can't, Hugh. I promised to keep Moira company—this is a worrying time for her. I can't just announce that I'm going out to dinner.'

'Make it later, then. Nine-thirty, say? They serve dinner till late at the Angel. Advise your friend to have an early night, it'll do her more good than sitting up till all hours talking. I'll meet you in the foyer.' Before she could reply he had walked past her and out through the doors of the coffee bar.

Corrie had no intention of suggesting an early night to Moira. If Hugh wanted to wait around in the hotel foyer that was his problem, she told herself. But as it happened Moira herself announced that she wanted to go to bed early. The girl looked pale and drawn. She was both physically and emotionally exhausted, and by the time Angus was asleep she was ready to fall into bed herself.

Corrie glanced at her watch as she travelled down in the lift. It was half past eight. With a bit of luck Hugh wouldn't have arrived yet and she'd miss him.

But she'd forgotten how persistent he could be once he had made up his mind to do something. As she walked through the hotel's swing doors he was the first person she saw. He sat waiting, a magazine on his lap. When he saw her he rose and came towards her, smiling.

'Good, you're early. I've booked a table.'

'Moira was tired, I... .'

He took her arm, smiling. 'Don't apologise. We'll have time for a drink now. The table's booked for nine o'clock.'

Gently but firmly, she shook off his hand. 'If you don't mind, I'd like to go up to my room and change,' she told him.

'Of course. I'll come with you.'

'*No!* Hugh, for heaven's sake will you give me some space?'

He was clearly surprised at her vehemence. For the first time his eyes were uncertain as he looked down at her. 'All right. I'll meet you in the bar in. . .' he looked at his watch, 'shall we say twenty minutes?'

'I'll be down as soon as I'm ready.' She walked off towards the lift.

'Well, tell me,' she said as they faced each other across the table half an hour later.

He glanced up from the menu he was studying. 'Tell you what?'

'What it is you want to talk to me about. What's the problem with Angus?'

'Angus?' He looked puzzled. 'Who's Angus?'

'Hugh, are you being deliberately obstructive? Angus Andrews, the child you're operating on tomorrow morning.'

'Oh, *that* Angus. There's no problem.'

She stared at him. 'But you told me you wanted to talk to me about him—led me to believe. . .'

'You *assumed*, you mean,' he interrupted. 'I'm sorry if you got the wrong idea. No, the child is in no danger. The operation is routine and perfectly straightforward.'

Corrie stared at him. 'Then why did you say you wanted to talk to me about him?'

He gave her the wry smile she remembered so well. 'I thought you might not come just to see me,' he explained. 'You see, I'm still unsure of myself—lacking in confidence.'

Corrie laughed in spite of herself. The last thing Hugh lacked was confidence. It had been one of the things that had attracted her to him. But what she had once seen as assertiveness and positivity now looked like brash insensitivity. As they ate she found herself noticing other things—looking at him almost as though he were a total stranger. For the first time she noticed the way he arranged his hair over the patch on top that was thinning, the slight heaviness around his jaw, and the suspicion of a paunch straining the waistband of his well cut trousers. For the first time she realised with a small shock that Hugh was old enough to be her father. The thought amused her.

Hugh looked up at her. 'You're smiling—that's better.' He drained his wine glass. 'Now, how about a brandy with your coffee?'

'I don't think so, thank you,' she said. 'I want to have a clear head for tomorrow.'

He raised an eyebrow at her. 'Anyone would think *you* were going to be in theatre! Or was that meant as a reproach?'

She shrugged. 'You know your own limitations better than I do. If you want to drink I'm sure you won't let me stop you.'

He hesitated, then waved the waiter away. 'You know, Corrie, you've changed,' he said at last. 'You've grown up. I'm not at all sure that it suits you.'

Looking across the table at him, she knew a sudden feeling of lightness deep inside and realised with a stab of joy that she was free—free of Hugh and free to be herself again, to live, even to love again; to do what she wanted with the rest of her life. She began to gather up her belongings. 'Thank you for the dinner, Hugh. I think I'll turn in now. Quite a day tomorrow.'

She saw him flush. 'Corrie, come back to me,' he said quietly.

She looked at him in surprise. 'That's out of the question.'

'You're still bitter. You're only saying that because you feel I let you down, but I'll make it up to you, I promise.'

'No. It's over, Hugh.'

'What about your career? You miss theatre work, admit it. You're a talented theatre sister. You're throwing yourself away up there in Glenhaggis or whatever the damned silly place is called.'

'Surely that's my affair?' She stood up. 'Goodnight, Hugh. Maybe I'll see you tomorrow.' She walked coolly out of the restaurant, leaving him staring after her.

The elated feeling was still with her when she got to her room. All these months she had been weighed down by memories of Hugh and what he had done to her. Now the heaviness was gone. She felt as new and as light as a bubble. And totally wide awake. How would she ever sleep? Sitting on the bed, she caught sight of the telephone. She'd ring William. Suddenly the one thing she wanted most in the world was to hear his voice. Picking up the receiver, she asked

Reception for an outside line and dialled the number. At the other end it rang three times, then clicked. William's voice said, 'Hello, Dr William Forbes here. I'm sorry I'm out on a call at the moment, but if you leave your name and number. . .'

She replaced the receiver with an almost overwhelming rush of disappointment. She'd wanted— no, *needed* to speak to William; to know he was still there. Now she would have to wait.

Angus was first on Hugh's list the following morning. Corrie was up early, taking a quick breakfast in her room, then hurrying across to the hospital. Moira was trying hard not to let Angus see how nervous she was. She looked even more tired than she had the previous night, and admitted to Corrie that she'd hardly slept a wink.

'Have you had breakfast?' Corrie asked.

Moira shook her head. 'I don't think I could eat anything, and anyway, I didn't want to leave him. He got so upset when the nurse gave him the injection.'

Angus looked tiny and defenceless in the theatre gown and cap, but Corrie could see the telltale signs that the pre-med injection was taking effect.

'You really should eat something,' she said. 'Go along and have a bite before they come for him. He's sleepy now, and I'll be here.'

Moira went off reluctantly to the canteen and Corrie sat down beside the dozing child. When the door opened a few minutes later she looked up, expecting to see a porter arriving to take Angus to the theatre. Instead Hugh stood there. He wore theatre greens and boots. Corrie got to her feet.

'Hugh, is something wrong?'

'I'm afraid there is. My scrub nurse has gone sick.'

'Isn't there someone who can take her place?'

'No one I'd trust. There's a heavy list in all the theatres this morning. Even on-take is in use, so staff is fully stretched. It looks as though I'm going to have to postpone my morning list.'

'But surely there must be some way. . .' Corrie broke off, her mouth suddenly dry as she realised why he was here. 'Oh, no, Hugh, I can't!'

'You *could*,' he said. 'In fact I'm relying on you, Corrie. I've told them to go ahead and get ready, because my London theatre sister is in the building. You're not going to let me down, are you?'

Corrie's head whirled. Moira was so keyed up. Angus had even had his pre-med. If he couldn't have his operation now—if they had to take him home again. . .

As though reading her thoughts, Hugh said, 'Corrie, I'm sure I don't have to tell you that if I don't operate today it could be another week—longer, even.'

'All right.' She stood up. 'Moira's having breakfast. She'll be back shortly. As soon as I've explained to her I'll come.'

He let out a sigh of relief. 'Thank goodness! I'll tell one of the nurses to bring you along to the surgery suite when you're ready. We'll be expecting you.'

Ten minutes later Corrie was scrubbing up in the nurses' changing-room, a young nurse standing by, waiting to help her on with the sterile gown and gloves and tie her mask. Sister bustled in and introduced herself briefly, then she showed Corrie where everything was. Corrie thanked heaven that all theatres were similar in pattern and design. As for the instruments used in cardio-vascular surgery, she was as familiar with those as she was with her own toothbrush. Together with Sister she laid out the instruments on the trolley, checking them off meticulously against the prepared list. Then, covered with sterile towels, they were wheeled into position. At Sister's signal the doors opened and the tiny anaesthetised patient was wheeled in, accompanied by the anaesthetist. Hugh came through the door from the surgeon's room, gowned and masked, gloved hands held aloft. His young registrar Gerald Jameson acknowledged Corrie, smiling at her over his mask as he took up his position next to Hugh. Two housemen and a small group of surgical students also took up their positions.

As Corrie took the forceps and lifted the towels covering the instruments for Hugh's inspection she glanced at the tiny, still figure on the table and offered up a silent prayer. Moira had shown touching confidence when she knew Corrie was going to be helping in the theatre.

'Don't worry about not staying with me,' she said. 'Now I know that you'll be there I'm not worried about Angus at all.' Corrie prayed that her confidence would be justified.

'Fine. All present and correct.' Hugh's eyes met hers across the operating table. He smiled. 'Quite like old times, isn't it?' He addressed his students as Sister folded back the sterile sheet, exposing the child's chest.

'First on our list this morning we have a four-year-

old male child suffering from a stenosis of the pulmo-
nary valve. I shall perform a valvotomy, a routine
procedure which should be straightforward and prove
completely successful.' He held out his hand to the
scrub nurse at his side. 'Right then, we'll begin—
scalpel.'

'Scalpel.' Corrie slapped the instrument firmly into
his outstretched hand.

As the last patient on the list was wheeled away to
the recovery-room the hands of the theatre clock stood
at one-thirty. Hugh peeled off his gloves and dropped
them into the bowl Sister held for him. He pulled
down his mask and smiled at Corrie.

'Thanks. It was a heavy morning. I owe you—and
so do the patients, if they only knew. But for you some
of them would have had to wait.'

'Glad I was here. It was good to see you at work
again, Hugh.' Already she was going through the
familiar routine, gathering up instruments and checking them with the list, preparing them for sterilisation.
'As soon as I'm through here I'd like to go and see
how Angus is.'

'Don't worry, the child will be fine. Tearing around
playing football before you know it!' He followed her
into the instrument-room. 'I always have coffee and
sandwiches sent up to my office after my morning list.
Join me?'

She shook her head. 'I came here to be with Moira
and Angus, and I've hardly spent any time with them
so far.'

'I'd say you'd done rather better than that. Another

ten minutes won't hurt—you've worked for it. I'll be in my office when you've changed.'

Corrie allowed him to walk away without arguing. There were things she needed to say to Hugh anyway.

He was sitting at his desk when she walked in, and he looked up with an approving smile.

'You look gorgeous! I always fancied you most without make-up. That scrubbed clean look is strangely sexy on you.'

She let the remark go. 'Hugh, thank you for asking me to scrub for you this morning. If I had any career doubts I've just laid them to rest.'

'That's interesting. Tell me more.'

'I know now that I want to work with *live* patients.'

He laughed. 'That's my aim too, oddly enough.'

'You know what I mean, Hugh. In theatre they're always unconscious. They never actually see us— well, me, anyway. Up in Glencarron I've been work-ing with people, learning to listen to them—getting to know more about the pyschology of illness. I know now that's where my real vocation is. I did think I missed theatre work—till today. Now my eyes are open.' She searched her mind for a way to make him see how she felt. 'It's the difference between— between building a boat and sailing it.'

He leaned back in his chair and regarded her for several minutes. 'Mmm, I seem to be hoist with my own petard, don't I? Tell me, would I be wrong in thinking there's someone you'd quite like to sail this love-boat of yours into the sunset with?' He chuckled softly at her telltale blush. 'I'm right, aren't I?' He got up and came across to put his hands on her shoulders. 'I might have known it wasn't me, making your eyes shine like that. Goodbye then, Corrie. And good luck. He's a damned lucky guy. I hope he's worth it.' He kissed her gently on the forehead. 'Send me a piece of wedding cake, eh?'

CHAPTER TEN

WHEN Corrie finally swung the Rover off the road on to the lochside track the following evening she felt the thrill of anticipation sing through her veins. The front door of Glencoe House was already open. Sheila, Kathy and Dr Walter came out on to the steps to greet her, eager for news of Angus. Although Corrie had telephoned them each evening from the hospital, first-hand news was what they wanted to hear.

Seated in the sitting-room with the golden rays of the evening sun slanting in through the window, she told them everything that had happened during the four days she had been away.

'And you say he's out of Intensive Care now?' Kathy asked anxiously.

'Yes. Back in his own room, breathing unaided and looking a different child already,' Corrie told her.

'And to think you actually assisted at the operation!' Sheila said.

Corrie smiled. 'That was just chance. I'm glad I happened to be there to help out in an emergency.'

Dr Walter patted her shoulder. 'Well done, my dear. We're all very proud of you.'

Corrie shook her head. 'It was nothing, just my job.' While she had been talking her eyes kept straying to the open doorway. Now she could contain herself no longer. 'Er—where's William?'

A look flashed between Sheila and Walter. 'He fully

intended to be here to welcome you, dear,' Sheila told her, 'but he was a little worried about old Morag. He telephoned to say he was going to take a look at her after surgery.'

'Is she ill?' asked Corrie anxiously.

'I'm afraid so,' Dr Walter said. 'He went to check her yesterday and found her in a poor way. He's quite concerned about her.' He looked at his watch. 'If you're not too tired why don't you drive over there? I'm sure he'd appreciate your help. Maybe you can even help him persuade the old soul to go to hospital.'

'Oh—well. . .' Corrie stood up, trying hard to keep the eager note out of her voice. 'Perhaps I will. I did try to ring him while I was away, but he was out.'

Driving up on to the moorland road, Corrie felt her weariness lift from her like a cloud. Something about the air—the magic *feel* of Glencarron put life and strength back into her. It felt like coming home. Or was it the thought of seeing William again? she asked herself. In her mind she rehearsed what she would say to him, phrasing and re-phrasing words that seemed suddenly trite and inadequate. Apprehension made her heart beat faster. Would her courage fail her? Could she bring herself to say it all when it actually came to the crunch? Was she taking too much for granted? Would it be what he wanted to hear?

She spotted William's red car gleaming in the sunlight as she rounded the bend on the narrow road. Parking the Rover behind it, she climbed the gate and began to walk across the stretch of moorland, but when she got to Morag's tumbledown croft she found it empty. Disappointed, she stood for a moment wondering what could have happened. Had William already taken Morag to hospital? But his car was still there, and no other vehicle had passed her on the road. Puzzled and a little concerned for the old woman, she searched the rugged landscape with her eyes. The moor and mountainside seemed deserted. Then something caught her attention. On the lower slopes of the mountain she could see a figure moving. From where she was it was impossible to tell whether it was male or female, adult or child. A sudden intuitive stab of urgency sent her running towards the mountain, stumbling over the tussocks of heather and then scrambling up the incline towards the wooded slope.

She climbed till she was out of breath. Pausing to look back, she could see Morag's croft far below, a thin trail of smoke rising from the chimney. There was no sign now of the figure she had seen. The trees and scrub had thinned out and above her rose the rocky shoulder of Craecuillin. She began to climb with difficulty, her unsuitable shoes slipping on the loose scree. After another few minutes she paused again to scan the surrounding ground. It was then that she spotted the crumpled figure lying a few yards away, partially hidden by bracken. At first she thought it was a bundle of rags, then she saw that it was an old woman—Morag. She was about to run towards her when a fox suddenly appeared out of the scrub. Corrie stood quite still, recognising the animal immediately by its damaged ear. It was Morag's fox, the one she had recently released after healing its broken leg. For a moment it stood motionless, nose twitching as it sniffed the air, one paw raised. Then slowly and stealthily it crept forward. Corrie watched in fascination as it began gently to lick Morag's face, clearly trying to revive her.

She neither saw nor heard the man till the shot rang out, making her spin round in alarm. The fox dropped, instantly dead at Morag's side. Gavin McLeod stood some forty feet away, releasing the spent cartridge from the barrel of his shotgun. As it dropped to the stony ground with a metallic clatter, something inside Corrie seemed to erupt. Tears stinging her eyes, she ran at him.

'Why did you do that? It was *her* fox. It sensed she was ill, and it wanted to help her.' She stood in front of him, her eyes blazing, too angry to think about what she was saying as, shaking with emotion, she shouted, 'You call yourself *Laird*? You'll never be a real laird till you learn to understand things like that. *Loyalty*—pure, instinctive loyalty, that's what you've just witnessed and misunderstood. This place—it's more than just a grouse moor and a mountain and a heap of old stones. It's people and creatures, air and earth. They are what matter. They are the life, the spirit of the place. Morag loved Glencarron in ways you'll never understand if you live to be a hundred!'

She turned from him and ran to where Morag lay. Sinking to her knees, she laid her hand against the old woman's chest. To her great relief she was still breathing. She turned back to Gavin, who stood looking on, his face stunned.

'No thanks to you she's still alive!' she shouted. 'Well, don't just stand there, help me with her, can't you? We have to do something!'

Gavin pointed. 'It's all right, the doctor's coming. I think it's best that we try to stay calm.'

Corrie felt relief overwhelm her as she looked up and saw William coming towards them along the path.

He acknowledged her briefly, then turned to Gavin. 'I heard a shot. What happened? Is anybody hurt?'

Gavin nodded towards Morag. 'I killed a fox—I thought it was going to attack her.' He looked at Corrie. 'Maybe you don't realise what scavengers they are,' he said. 'They're quite capable of. . .'

'Of *surviving*—if they're not shot, trapped or gassed,' she finished his sentence bitterly. 'And there are some among us who'd like to polish off people in the same way.' Knowing she was letting her anger get the better of her, she took a deep breath and looked up at William. Morag was their priority now. 'She's still breathing, but only just. Can we carry her down safely?'

William sank to his knees and lifted one of the old woman's limp, fragile arms, feeling for the weak, thready pulse. Meeting Corrie's anxious eyes, he shook his head. 'She doesn't have long, I'm afraid. Best let her rest. It's pneumonia. I knew it yesterday, but there was nothing I could do. It's my guess she came up here to die, close to nature the way her friends the animals do.'

Corrie was taking off her scarf, making a pillow to slip under Morag's head. 'I'd like to stay with her till—till. . .'

He nodded. 'Yes, of course.'

Gavin stepped closer. 'Is there anything I can do?'

'God only knows how she found the strength to get

up here,' William said. 'But it's going to be a problem getting her down.'

Gavin nodded. 'If you came back with me now we could fetch a hurdle or something. We could carry her between us.'

William glanced at Corrie. 'Will you be all right here for a while if I go? There's nothing more I can do for her now. I doubt if she'll regain consciousness again.'

Corrie watched them go with a feeling of sadness and desolation. This wasn't the way she had visualised her homecoming at all. The sun disappeared behind the mountain top, etching its outline in blood red against the sky. A wind sprang up and the evening air felt suddenly chill and unfriendly. There was no sound except for the distant cry of a curlew and the soft rustling of the wind stirring the bracken. She laid a hand on Morag's cheek. It felt cold and clammy. Slipping off her jacket, she tucked it round the old woman's shoulders in a desperate attempt to bring comfort. As she did so the sharp black eyes opened and looked up at her, startling her with their clarity and alertness. Seeing the dry lips move, Corrie leaned forward to catch the whispered words.

'He'll be braw gi'en time, lassie,' Morag said. 'He'll mak' a laird yet—when he learns ye canna fight Nature—and win.'

'I'll tell him, Morag, I promise.' Corrie took the cold hand in hers and held it, but as she did so old Morag smiled and closed her eyes again. A moment later the shallow breathing came to a peaceful stop.

Very tenderly Corrie covered her with the jacket, a tight knot of tears in her throat. When she looked up again she saw Gavin and William striding quickly across the moor, carrying a hurdle between them.

The ambulance that William had telephoned for was waiting on the moorland road. As it moved away, followed by Gavin's Land Rover, William took off his jacket and slipped it round Corrie's shoulders. 'You're shivering. Better come back with me. I'll make you a hot drink, or maybe you'd like something stronger.'

She looked up at him. 'Thanks, I would like a drink,' she said shakily.

'I heard what you said to McLeod,' he told her, holding her cold hands warmly in both of his. 'It was quite a speech. I was very proud of you.'

'I'm afraid I was terribly rude, but I couldn't help it.' She swallowed hard, but when he put his arms around her and drew her close she could hold back the tears no longer. Leaning against him, she sobbed against his chest as though her heart would break. He let her cry for a few minutes, then shook her gently.

'Hey, come on! This isn't like you. Morag was very old and she was ready to go. We should be glad for her that she went as she always wanted to, up here in the place she loved best.'

Later, as she sat in William's study, sipping the stiff malt whisky he poured for her, Corrie said,

'I'm sorry about the tears, William. I've seen people die before and I haven't allowed myself to get emotionally involved. But it's been a traumatic few days.'

He took a seat beside her on the chesterfield. 'With Angus, you mean?'

'Yes, but not entirely.' She looked at him. 'William,

there's something I have to tell you. At the hospital I discovered that the consultant setting up the new heart unit was Hugh Davies—my ex. . .' She broke off, seeing his wry smile. 'William? You—*knew*?'

'Well, guessed might be a little more accurate. I knew an eminent cardiologist from your old hospital was setting up the unit. You'd mentioned the name Hugh. It wasn't too difficult to put two and two together.'

'And yet you let me—no, *asked* me to go?'

'I've always known that he wasn't completely out of your system. It was important to me to have you see him again.'

'*Why*, William?'

'Isn't it obvious? Because I damn well *love* you, of course,' he said vehemently. 'I told you I'd ask you to marry me just once more. Lord knows why I said that. The old male pride rearing its head, I suppose. But having given myself just one more chance I wanted to be sure that if you said yes you'd mean it.'

'So you set me up? But suppose I'd decided to go back to Hugh?'

'That was the risk I had to take. It would have hurt like hell, of course, but it would have proved once and for all that I was just a rebound thing for you.' His voice was husky as he added, 'You see, Corrie, I need all of you—not just half. I'm enough of a male chauvinist to want to be the most important person in your life. I couldn't settle for less.'

She felt her heart contract. 'But when I told you about Hugh, you said you knew how I felt. I got the impression that your heart had taken a battering too—that *I* would be second best.'

'*Second best?*' He stared at her incredulously. 'Don't you know that it was only ever you I wanted, Corrie? Ever since I can remember you were the girl who haunted my dreams and made all the others look dull by comparison. Although I hadn't learned to read my own emotions at the time, I know now that it was wanting you so badly that made me such a monster when we were growing up. I resented the way you enslaved me and twisted my heart.' He smiled wryly. 'Now you're learning all my secrets. Does any of it make sense?' He drew her close. 'You'll never know the misgivings I suffered after I'd sent you back into his arms. In fact, if you really want to know, I haven't slept a wink since you left here. Can you picture how it was—imagining the two of you together, your rapturous reunion; seeing you in his arms? Then when I heard that you'd been asked to assist him in theatre I was really worried. The man *and* the job you once loved. God, a pretty potent mixture!' He drew back his head to look down at her. 'So—do I get to hear the verdict? How much longer are you going to keep me in suspense?'

Thoughtfully Corrie laid her palm against his, lacing her fingers through his one by one. 'Well, to begin with, it shook me, seeing Hugh again suddenly like that. He asked me to have dinner with him and he told me that he and his wife had parted.' She squeezed his hand. 'But it didn't take long to find that everything I ever felt for him was totally dead. As for working in the theatre, I realised that the work I've done here these past months—getting to know people, helping them as individual human beings and not just sick bodies—that's what I really want.'

'I see. And is that all?'

She turned to look at him. 'No. There was more, something much more important. It hit me like an avalanche. I even tried to ring and tell you about it, but you were out on a call.'

'Damn! That proves how much I need that car phone.' He pulled her into his arms and held her tightly. 'Corrie, I appreciate the dramatic suspense, but I suppose you know you're driving me mad, don't you? Do I get to hear about this discovery of yours now, or do I have to squeeze it out of you?'

She wrapped her arms tightly round him, nuzzling her face into his neck contentedly. 'You know quite well what it is, don't you? I discovered that it's *you* I love, William. Discovered is the wrong word really, because I've known for a long time. Unlike you, I was well aware of it all those years ago. You broke my heart then and I vowed I'd never forgive you. But almost from the moment we met again the magic was there. This time it was me who tried to fight it.' She smiled, remembering something. 'Morag told me that you can't fight nature and win. She was right.'

'Who the hell wants to win, in this case? I surrender, happily and unconditionally.' He kissed her, gently at first, then passionately, giving way to all the pent-up fears and hunger he had felt since sending Corrie back into Hugh's arms. Corrie responded with all her heart, releasing all the love she had fought and suppressed over the past weeks, trying to tell him something words were too pale and inadequate to say.

For a while they stayed like that, content to be close, holding and caressing, oblivious to the world outside, aware only of each other and the beating of their hearts, one against the other.

At last William moved, easing his arm out from behind her. 'I suppose we should go and see Sheila and Dad,' he said reluctantly. 'They'll be wondering where we've got to.'

She stirred drowsily against his shoulder. 'I suppose we must.'

He looked down at her. 'It's very hard to let you go when you look at me like that.' He sat up, frowning suddenly. 'Of course, you realise, don't you, that you might well have blown the whole thing?'

'What do you mean?' she queried.

'Well, it's still the custom in Glencarron to ask the Laird's permission to marry.' He shook his head doubtfully. 'And after what you said to him this evening. . .' He looked at her gravely and for a moment she was taken in, then she saw the twitching at the corners of his mouth and picking up a cushion she swung it at him.

'William Forbes, you never change! You're as bad as ever!'

'You're right—I am.' He pulled her to her feet and hugged her to him hard. 'I'll never change, and I hope you won't either.' He ran a hand down her back and drew her closer. 'Mmm, you feel so good, Corrie—so right in my arms. It's where you belong.' He glanced down at her with a wry smile. 'And now we really must go, before I lose control completely.'

'William. . .?' she queried.

'Yes?'

'Haven't you forgotten something?'

For a second he looked puzzled, then light dawned. 'Do I really have to ask you?'

'You won't get an answer unless you do.'

Very gravely he took her hand. 'Corrie Ashley, please will you marry me? And you'd better say yes, unless you want to be held prisoner in this house all night.'

She stood on tiptoe to wind her arms around his neck, her eyes sparkling up into his. 'Would that be a proposal or a proposition, Dr Forbes? Either way, the answer is *yes*!'

Sheila and Dr Walter were married in the register office at Glencarron Town Hall two weeks later, with Corrie and William as witnesses and chief guests. Back at Glencoe House Kathy had prepared a delicious wedding breakfast for friends of the couple and patients of Dr Walter. It was after William had toasted the happy couple that Dr Walter got to his feet.

'And now I'd like to propose a toast to another couple,' he said. 'In a month's time I'm to acquire a new daughter-in-law.' He smiled at Corrie. 'And not before time, I might say, because for me, it's a very long-term dream come true.' He lowered his voice conspiratorially. 'And now I'll tell you all a secret. Believe it or not, these two young people actually wanted to have a quiet double ceremony along with Sheila and me today. Well, Sheila and I knew that the people of Glencarron would never stand for that, and I was right, wasn't I?' A shout of approval went up. Dr Walter raised his voice above it: 'So you're all invited to the wedding of the year a month today. It's to be at St Duncan's Church and the bride will be dressed in a beautiful white dress. It's a sure thing that she'll be one of the bonniest you've seen in a long time.' He grinned mischievously across the room at William. 'A pity I can't say the same for the groom, but I'm sure he'll do his best to look appealing in his full Highland rig.' He held his glass high. 'So shall we drink to the future Mrs Forbes—or *Mrs Doctor*, as she's bound to be called? The first "Mrs Doctor" Glencarron has had for many a year. And high time too.'

William raised his glass to Corrie's and made her a silent promise with his eyes as the joyful toast went round the room:

'To Dr William and the future Mrs Forbes.'

As William bent to kiss his future bride he whispered in her ear, 'I love you—*Mrs Doctor*.'

4 MEDICAL ROMANCES
AND 2 FREE GIFTS
From Mills & Boon

Capture all the excitement, intrigue and emotion of the busy medical world by accepting four FREE Medical Romances, plus a FREE cuddly teddy and special mystery gift. Then if you choose, go on to enjoy 4 more exciting Medical Romances every month! Send the coupon below at once to:

MILLS & BOON READER SERVICE, FREEPOST PO BOX 236, CROYDON, SURREY CR9 9EL.
No stamp required

✂ - ✂

YES! Please rush me my 4 Free Medical Romances and 2 Free Gifts! Please also reserve me a Reader Service Subscription. If I decide to subscribe, I can look forward to receiving 4 Medical Romances every month for just £6.40, delivered direct to my door. Post and packing is free, and there's a free Mills & Boon Newsletter. If I choose not to subscribe I shall write to you within 10 days - I can keep the books and gifts whatever I decide. I can cancel or suspend my subscription at any time. I am over 18.

EP19D

Name (Mr/Mrs/Ms) _____

Address _____

_____

_____ Postcode _____

Signature _____

mps
MAILING
PREFERENCE
SERVICE